ANNE

1881-
1882

PRAIRIE ROSES
COLLECTION FIVE
BOOK 27

RENA GROOT

This book is mostly a work of fiction. References to historical events, real people, or real places are used fictitiously, for the most part. Most names, places, characters, and events are products of the author's imaginations. There are some resemblances to actual events or places or persons, living or dead. It is not entirely coincidental.

First Edition April 26, 2023

Printed and bound in the United States of America

ISBN: 9798385765843

Cover art by Randi Gammons of Randi Gammons Graphic Design
Branding for series by Chatona Having
Editing by my beautiful ARC readers
Formatting by Delia Latham

Dedication

I fully realize everything we have is a gift from God.
We can do nothing and we have nothing apart from Him.
I am thankful He gave me a love (okay, an addiction) for writing.
Lord God, I dedicate this book to You for Your glory.

I also dedicate Anne to my beautiful daughters,
Sarah Beth, Shalev Alice, and Savannah Evelyn.
Anne, this amazing spunky woman,
reminds me of the three of you.

*May the Lord ♡
bless and keep
you ~ today
and forever!
Love,
Rena ♡ Troot
(Word ♡)*

TABLE OF CONTENTS

Dedication

CHAPTER ONE

Anne smiled as if she was guarding some delicious secret. She could never have imagined she'd be married and traveling over two thousand miles in a covered wagon. The very thought of being a mail-order bride once sounded so ludicrous. She'd been so frightened about it at first. Her mother said the very idea of marrying someone she had never met was complete insanity. But, traveling these three months beside her husband, basking in his love . . .

Her William proved to be more than she could have asked for. He was tall and handsome, a perfect man, well . . . near perfect. No one but Jesus was perfect.

"I'm so glad you insisted we marry back in Independence on the very day I arrived."

"Didn't want you to change your mind."

"Who wouldn't want to marry you?" She giggled, adjusting her bonnet.

As they stopped to set up camp for the night, Anne jumped from the wagon and froze where she landed. She couldn't move. The beauty surrounding her was mesmerizing. The hills were ablaze with gold and scarlet from the setting sun. The wind softly blew wisps of hair across her face. She breathed in the sweet smell of the prairie grass that rippled around her like ocean waves. There seemed to be no end to the sky. It looked like a window into eternity. Anne watched William blow on the kindling to start the evening fire. Baby flames leaped into the air. Coyotes started their evening serenade, crying to God for their supper. It was all so breathtakingly beautiful. She had never felt so happy, so content, in all her life.

Anne was thankful William gave her time to breathe in the beauty. He didn't scold her, as others would have, and demand she get supper ready. Looking towards the lingering colors of the setting sun, Anne was surprised to see the captain and two men loping towards them from the back of the wagon train.

"Hmmm, I wonder what that's all about?" she questioned aloud.

Her husband followed her gaze. His stare turned into a glare before her eyes. There was something she had never seen in those green eyes before. The cold ugliness almost stopped her heart.

"Anne, get in the wagon." An unfamiliar meanness edged his voice.

"Why? Is something wrong?"

"Do as I say!" The tone of his voice scared her.

"Yes, William."

The strangers reined in their mounts as they approached William's wagon.

Anne hesitated. "But what's the matter?"

"Now! Just do it!" he hissed through clenched teeth.

Hurrying to the back of the wagon, she took one last glance before grabbing hold of the ladder and hiking herself up. What could the captain and those men want? Why had William acted that way? She peeked around the corner of the canvas and was shocked to see her husband pull his pistol. Gunshots echoed through the air. Her husband lay crumpled on the ground. Anne climbed out of the wagon as fast as she could and ran to him.

"William!" A crimson stain spread across the front of his shirt. She glared at the strangers. "What have you done?" She put her hand on his chest. It remained perfectly still. There was no breath. She looked at his face. His eyes stared into nothingness. Her husband was dead.

"No! Nooooo! William, no! God, help me!"

Sobs racked her body as she collapsed onto his corpse.

The next thing Anne knew, strong hands gripped her shoulders and pulled her away from William.

"No! Leave me alone!"

"I'm sorry, ma'am. I didn't have a choice."

She glared up into the man's face. "Didn't have a choice? Are you crazy? You just murdered my husband!" She turned to the captain. "You saw what happened. You can't let him get away with this!"

"Ma'am, he's a US Marshal."

Anne couldn't believe what just happened. She was finally having a life of her own—freedom and a husband. She was soon to have her very own home in California. Now this? Widowed and alone on the Oregon Trail.

God, what were You thinking? I thought I could trust You.

Anne slumped onto a stump beside the now blazing fire. She couldn't stop sobbing. The marshal sat on a stump beside the widow, trying to calm her.

"I'm sorry for your loss, Ma'am."

Anne screamed inside her head at this wretched man. *Shut up! You aren't sorry at all!*

It was surprising how quickly hatred could consume the human heart. She now hated the marshal. Why did he shoot her husband? She would never forgive him.

The captain had to know why this happened. He led the marshal and his deputy right to William. Everything happened so fast. If they hadn't drawn their guns, would the story have been different?

This whole thing seemed like a nightmare and Anne felt

trapped in it. Watching the deputy pull a shovel off the side of the wagon was surreal. The deputy strode off to dig a grave. The captain followed—her husband's body draped over a horse.

How could that be her husband's body? How could he be dead? There must be some mistake. She had just spoken to him. Anne stared at the fire William had just built—still burning brightly—as if nothing happened. Tears stung her eyes.

Lord, make this horrible man—this murderer—go away—leave me alone.

Anne couldn't tell him to go away. She was crying so hard the words caught in her throat and wouldn't come out. She didn't want to hear his words, but the marshal insisted on talking to her.

He repeated, "I'm sorry for your loss, ma'am."

Does he think I didn't hear him before? Or maybe he's just plain stupid and has no other words to say. Make him shut up, Lord. Better yet, could you send a few lightning bolts his way and strike him dead?

They sat for over an hour, listening to the sound of the shovel turning the earth. The horrible sound finally stopped, and the captain walked over to the fire. He gave the marshal a nod. "A word?"

They moved a stone's throw away. Did they really think she couldn't hear them? It's funny how sounds carry on the prairie at night.

"I can't have an unaccompanied woman on my train. It would be too dangerous."

The hard reality of her situation settled over Anne's shoulders like a cold blanket.

Now what, God? Do You have a plan or are You just going to send me off to die in the wilderness?

The marshal's voice sounded thoughtful. "Couldn't a few of the men on the train take shifts to help her?"

"Never work. She can't pull her weight. There'd be fighting over her, and there'd be men who'd try to force their attentions on her. Way too much trouble. She can't stay."

The coyote's howling suddenly hushed—as if they held their breath—waiting to hear what would be said next.

"I have an idea." The marshal spoke so quietly Anne had to strain to hear his words.

"We passed Fort Laramie a couple days ago. I'm headed back that way. My deputy and I could take her there. There are families there—womenfolk. She wouldn't be alone."

"Well, that sounds like a mighty fine solution. I'll tell her she's leaving with you—that you're pulling out first thing in the morning."

The captain strolled towards her. Did he really expect her to travel with that horrid man—that murderer?

"Ma'am. I'm sorry—but, I'm afraid you can't continue to Oregon alone on this train. The marshal has offered to take you back to Fort Laramie."

Anne said nothing. She didn't trust herself to say anything. Her thoughts were too horrible.

"He will be pulling out in the morning. He has offered to drive your team."

Anne's mouth went dry. Her body seemed frozen to the spot. Words tumbled through her mind— but she couldn't make them come out. She couldn't believe the feelings trying to encase her heart and hold her hostage. Hatred. Bitterness. Unforgiveness. Revenge.

First, God took her husband. Now, did He really expect her to travel with her husband's murderer? Did God love her at all?

The next morning, Anne walked far behind the man walking beside her oxen. She despised this man.

The marshal called back, "You're welcome to rest in the wagon if you get tired, ma'am."

His intentions were good, but she didn't want his help. She wanted to be walking beside William. Maybe, with any luck, the marshal would trip and break his neck.

Anne walked for about an hour. The sun beat down on her mercilessly. She had barely slept the night before. Physically and emotionally exhausted, Anne climbed into the back of the wagon. It was so full of supplies there was hardly any room to sleep. She wedged herself into a corner, but the pitching of the wagon made sleep impossible. She tossed for a few hours, as the wagon jolted over bumps and rocks.

God, I know it's not right, but I hate him. I will never forgive him. Don't ever ask me to forgive him.

Anne gave up trying to rest, climbed out of the wagon, and again walked a good distance behind the marshal. They followed the deep grooves made from other wagons near the banks of the Platte River.

He called back to her, "Couldn't rest?"

"How'd you figure that out?"

"You just missed the biggest herd of buffalo I've ever seen."

Anne didn't answer. He didn't deserve an answer. She watched the tall prairie grasses swaying in the hot breeze. It was so dusty. The prairie stretched as far as she could see. The dazzling blue sky seemed to go on forever.

The marshal called back to her, "The breeze is fairly calm now, but it's not always this calm. Winds sometimes howl through this land with such force wagon canvases are shredded."

Anne ignored his comment.

When they stopped for lunch of hard biscuits, bison jerky, and sweet tea, Anne continued to ignore the marshal. Maybe if she pretended he wasn't there, he would be quiet and the trip would go faster? Ignoring him didn't help. He didn't seem to be able to take a hint. He kept talking.

"Ma'am, I've made this trip a few times. It would be dangerous for you to be alone on the Oregon Trail."

Well, if he wanted to talk, she would talk about important things. "Why did you shoot William?"

"I had no choice ma'am. It was him or me."

"That's not what I meant. Why would you shoot an innocent man?"

"I'd rather not say at this time, ma'am."

"Why? Is it because you have no good reason?"

"I think you've had enough grief for one day, ma'am."

There was no way of dragging an answer out of him, so after the brief lunch Anne let him walk ahead again so she could be alone with her thoughts.

Hours later, with no civilization in sight, and the day drawing to a close, the marshal called back to her, "Well, this looks like a good spot to camp." He stopped the oxen.

"I'll see to the animals. Can you start a fire?"

"Can't anyone?"

Mosquitoes descended in droves at dusk. Anne swatted at them while she tried to prepare supper. She thought Pharaoh would have let the children of Israel go sooner if these mosquitoes had swarmed him.

Anne boiled the potatoes and jerky in a cauldron over a blazing fire. Hundreds of coyotes were yipping and howling in the distance. The marshal nursed a coffee and asked, "How are you doing, ma'am?

She pretended not to hear the question.

The deputy spoke up. "I'm truly sorry for your loss, Ma'am."

"You should be."

After dinner, the deputy went for a walk.

The marshal said, "I'm truly sorry for your loss, ma'am. I hope you can forgive me."

Forgive him? Was he crazy?

She knew if she didn't forgive, God wouldn't forgive her either, but she just couldn't.

She watched the flames dance in the deadfall she had collected. Embers exploded, sending tiny fireworks flying into the night sky.

Anne thought about what a funny thing time is. Yesterday at this time, she had a husband and was looking forward to building a home and a life with him. A day later she sat with two strangers— off in the wilds—with no husband. How quickly things change.

Several verses from the Bible flitted through her mind.

…whereas you do not know what will happen tomorrow. For

what is your life? It is even a vapor that appears for a little time and then vanishes away." [1]

William had no idea when he woke up yesterday morning that it would be the last day he had to breathe on Earth. If he had known, would he have done anything differently? Anne thought about how none of us knows the day we will stand before God.

"Take therefore no thought for the morrow: for the morrow shall take thought for the things of itself. Sufficient unto the day is the evil thereof." [2]

It certainly has been an evil day, Lord. Would You please avenge my husband's death? Could you please kill that marshal? You know, the eye for an eye thing You spoke about in Your Word. He shot an innocent man. He doesn't deserve to live.

"You owe me an explanation. Why did you shoot my husband?"

"Not today, ma'am," the marshal said as he climbed under the wagon for the night.

Anne almost screamed "You insufferable man! How dare you kill my husband and not tell me why!"

Instead, she held her tongue—and went to bed dreaming about how she could avenge William's death.

---

[1] James 4:14
[2] Matthew 6:34

CHAPTER TWO

It was torture trying to sleep that night. The insects sang in Anne's ears until dawn.

The next morning the marshal had coffee and cornmeal mush ready before Anne even woke up. As they sat by the fire he asked, "How are you this morning?"

Anne had no idea how to answer.

It was a simple question, but the answer seemed elusive.

The only thing she could think of to say was, "How am I? Why do you care?"

"Do you want to talk or be left alone?"

"Leave me alone…"

The rest of breakfast was eaten in silence.

Hoss, the deputy, rarely raised his eyes above the ground. He barely spoke, so it startled Anne when he said, "The fire's out. I'll pour water on it."

"Thanks, Hoss. The oxen are yoked to go. Are you ready to travel, Anne?"

"Yes"

Anne climbed onto the wagon bench. She wanted to ride for a bit and just admire the scenery.

The marshal goaded the oxen and called. "Hey now doggies, let's go!" The oxen obediently plowed forward. How they could carry thousands of pounds of weight for hours each day was a mystery to Anne.

They continued down the trail in silence. The grassland slowly morphed into stretches of desert, sand dunes, sagebrush, and huge rocky pinnacles. Anne wondered if they were travelling in circles. Everything looked the same. It was all so monotonous.

Being with that wretched man is so grievous, Lord. I can't bear this for at least another two months. Two minutes is too long. Are there any other options to get to California than to travel with that man?

As they sat around the campfire eating lunch, Anne was horrified to see the marshal pull out his pistol and aim it at his deputy.

What is this man doing? She squeezed her eyes shut. There was an explosion of gunfire and then silence. Anne was afraid to open her eyes. *Oh God, why have you sent me out in the wilds with this madman?*

She hesitantly opened her eyes, and was shocked to see the deputy sitting on a stump grinning. A huge rattlesnake lay dead at his feet.

"That was quick shooting, marshal. I'm obliged."

The marshal smiled. "Just sparing the life of a good man."

Ugly thoughts raced through her mind. She wished the marshal had sat on that snake.

The marshal seemed deep in thought. Finally, he looked at Anne and blurted out of nowhere, "Southeast Wyoming seems to stretch on forever—endless miles of flat land."

Why this man didn't give up trying to talk to her was a mystery.

"They call this big sky country. It goes all the way from Montanna."

Silence.

"There's a gentle slope for weeks before folks traveling West face a long, slow climb to the Rocky Mountains."

Anne didn't answer.

She walked behind the wagon for the rest of the afternoon, wrestling with God about her thoughts.

Lord, You said the heart of man is desperately wicked. I never saw the wickedness of my own heart before. I see it now. It's ugly. I know You can't forgive me if I don't forgive. Would you please change my heart? I can't do this on my own. I don't want to miss Heaven on account of this horrible marshal. I still pray You would murder him, as he murdered my William. Amen.

Arriving at Fort Laramie at dusk, Anne was exhausted from walking in the choking dust. Kindly settlers greeted them and took them in, let them scrub off the grime of the trail, and gave them a hot supper. Deer stew never tasted so good.

Anne glanced around the huge room. This was obviously the main dining room. There were twenty well-oiled pine tables with benches, each bench capable of seating about ten folks. The room was empty and dark, except for the oil lamp that burned brightly on their table.

They sat close to the hearth. The fire spread a warm welcome over the weary travelers. The evening had cooled off considerably. It was funny how the scorching hot prairie could be freezing cold at night.

Some folks were curious about this odd little group and hoped to find out more.

"Most folks around here go to bed when the sun goes down— but this is special. It isn't every day the fort has a US marshal, his deputy, and a beautiful young woman stop by. So, where are y'all from?" one of the soldiers asked. It was obvious no one else in the room existed in his eyes but Anne.

All eyes turned towards her. Anne blushed. She didn't like being the center of attention. All present seemed to be waiting for her answer.

"I'm from Independence, Missouri."

11

The man smiled. It was a strange smile. His eyes looked like a dog's eyes when he'd cornered a coon. The marshal seemed to have noticed, because he tried to divert the man's attention by saying, "I'm from Nebraska." The man asking the question didn't care. He kept staring at Anne.

The marshal asked, "Can someone tell us about this fort?"

An elderly man spoke up. "The name's Jeb. What's your name, son?"

The marshal smiled and said, "Logan, sir."

"Logan. That's a fine name," Jeb said.

I despise that name now, Anne thought.

"Well, Logan, I'm glad you asked. This here's an army outpost with a bakery, a telegraph station, officers and soldiers' quarters. There's nearly two hundred officers and soldiers here. There's a huge mercantile too. Folks can buy just about anything."

The soldier kept staring at Anne. The old man glared at the soldier, but nothing seemed to divert his attention. He continued, "We're at the meeting of the Laramie and North Platte Rivers. This here fort was started as a fur trading post back in the 1830s. I was a little gaffer then…"

The man stopped to take a deep draw of smoked sweetgrass from his corncob pipe.

"The US Army purchased the fort from the Indians about 1849. They must have figured they had to. So many folks on the trail saw bandits cropping up behind bushes and boulders. The Army needed forts to keep folks safe—a place to replenish goods, repair wagons, and find medical help if needed. This fort is a favorite stopping spot for migrants and thieves on the Oregon Trail."

"There's a spot for you in the barn, sir." The soldier didn't take his eyes off Anne as he spoke. "There's a spare room in the fort for you, ma'am." His eyes had an ugly gleam. "It's in the soldiers' quarters, right next to my room—so I can protect you, little lady. There's some rough men here."

Anne tried not to show her horror at this proposal. She didn't want to be anywhere near this man. There was something about him that made her skin crawl—it was what she imagined it would feel like if a thousand June bugs were trying to land on her at once.

A woman, who looked to be in her mid-thirties, spoke up. "My name's Grace. I have an empty bed in my room. You're welcome to bunk with me."

Relief washed over Anne. "Thank you, ma'am. My name's Anne. I'd be grateful to share a room with you."

Anne glanced at the soldier. His face had a surly look—like a child's face who had his hand on a desired toy only to have it snatched from his hand. He muttered something under his breath and stormed out of the room. Somehow, when he was gone, the air seemed easier to breathe.

Grace spoke again. "I don't know how long God will have you stay here, Anne, but it would be mighty nice to have more hands in the bakery. I have a hard time keeping up."

"I'd be happy to help you, Grace." Anne had no idea what God's plans were. They could be leaving tomorrow for all she knew. All her plans were now in a burn pile. If she hoped to go west, it seemed she was now dependent on the marshal.

That night, Anne tried to push thoughts of revenge out of her mind. She went to sleep repeating a verse she had memorized as a child. "*Search me, O God, and know my anxious thoughts.*"[3] She didn't want to hate the marshal…but she did. She wished he would die.

By the time Anne woke up, sunshine was already pouring through the lattice. She quickly dressed and splashed cold water on her face from a pitcher on the nightstand.

Walking into the main room was a shock. It was filled with men. Loud men. Their voices made it sound like there were many more than two hundred. As soon as Anne entered, there was a hush. All eyes turned towards her.

Anne smiled nervously. "Which way to the bakery?" Over two hundred fingers pointed towards a room Anne hadn't noticed

---

[3] Psalm 129:23

before.

"Thank you."

As she left the room, the noise was deafening.

"Good morning, Grace. I'm here to help you."

"Oh, thank God. I had no idea how I was going to get all the baking and washing done today."

"How can I help?"

"Would you like to bake or wash clothes?"

"I'd love to bake."

"You can make cornbread. The recipe is so easy and delicious. I never seem to make enough of it."

Grace handed Anne a paper with the recipe scribbled on it.

"Just follow the directions. All the ingredients are on the shelf behind you."

Anne read the directions out loud. "...Start with melting shortening in a cast iron skillet. Mix together cornmeal, flour, buttermilk, eggs, salt, baking powder and baking soda. Pour the batter into the melted shortening and bake it on the stove top."

"Easy, right? You'll get the hang of it."

"Let me see. Six tablespoons of shortening, one cup of cornmeal, one half cup all-purpose flour, one teaspoon salt, one cup buttermilk, one half cup milk, one egg, one tablespoon baking powder, and one-half teaspoon baking soda. Bake for twenty-five minutes or until the top is golden brown. Sounds easy enough."

"That will be your job all day. By dinner time you should have enough Johnny cakes to serve with the deer stew from yesterday...hopefully, at least one hundred cakes."

When Anne heard one hundred cakes, she prayed God would give her strength.

"Thank you, Anne. I'm grateful God sent you."

Anne grabbed a sack of cornmeal off the shelf. It was unfortunate the last person who used it forgot to tie it closed. Somehow, the sack fell sideways and Anne was covered in cornmeal. It covered her blonde hair, her face, her shoulders...

Lord, did that really have to be the moment the marshal walked by the bakery door?

Anne strode out of the room as graciously as possible under the circumstances. She forgot there were almost two hundred men sitting in the dining room. All talking ceased. All eyes were on Anne. There was a surprised moment of silence, then hysterical laughter filled the room. Anne had never felt so embarrassed. She passed by the men as if she didn't notice anything out of the usual.

Cleaning up the cornmeal was harder than she imagined. Brushing her hair kept revealing more meal.

A short time later, when she was sure the main hall was clear of smirking soldiers, she snuck back into the bakery. Grace was still laughing. Anne couldn't help it—she burst out laughing too. It helped relieve some of the anxiety that had built around her heart.

Stoking the wood fire and baking all day was almost more than Anne could bear. She slumped in a chair in the dining room in the late afternoon, completely exhausted.

I don't know what's wrong with me, but I can't do this every day, Lord. I have no energy. Help me. A verse came to Anne's heart. *"Come to me, all you who are weary and burdened, and I will give you rest. Take my yoke upon you and learn from Me, for I am gentle and humble in heart, and you will find rest for your souls. For My yoke is easy and My burden light."* [4]

Lord, I believe Your Word is true. I am so weary. Please give me Your rest.

---

[4] Matthew 11:28-30

CHAPTER THREE

Fort Laramie, Wyoming
June 1881

Anne was asked to bake all night so the bread would be ready for the hungry soldiers in the mornings. The baking seemed to go on forever. Why did the nights seem so long? She was beyond exhausted. She wasn't sure how she would survive.

Anne had been on the night shift for about a week. That night, while the next batch of bread baked, Anne sat by the fire in the dining room. She sunk into a chair at one of the tables, completely oblivious to her surroundings. She lay her head on the table, and was startled to hear, "Well, well, well. Look who just dropped by to say hello."

Anne glanced up at the soldier and tried to keep her expression neutral, but her heart said, "Oh no! Not you!"

"The name's Clayton. What's yours?"

"Anne."

"Anne." He spoke her name as if he was tasting it.

He's so repulsive, Lord. Please make him go away.

"So, what brings you to Fort Laramie, little lady?"

Anne leaped off the bench as if a snake bit her. "Oh gosh! I just remembered I have bread in the oven. I need to attend to it. Excuse me."

Anne fled from the room, nearly running over the marshal. "Sorry. Bread's in the oven..."

The marshal laughed and moved out of Anne's way. "There's some cornmeal on your shoulder," he called out. Anne paid no attention but hurried on as if she hadn't heard him.

Finally, thankfully, the bugle sounded. It was time for the soldiers to go to bed. They would be up at 4:00 am for a training exercise. Anne glanced up from preparing the next batch of dough. She was relieved to see Clayton leave—then revolted to see him blow her a kiss as he left the room. Anne shuddered as she said under her breath, "Horrid man."

Anne tried to sleep that night but scenes from the past kept her awake. Her heart was breaking. How could she move forward? She felt like a prisoner—held hostage in a horrible dream. It had all happened so quickly. Why were there no warning signs—no chance to flee from everything that happened—no way to prevent the inevitable?

Anne desperately wanted to escape the bitter prison she was locked in. She wondered if there would ever be peace or closure. It seemed like a lifetime ago the nightmare began. It was unfathomable God let William be killed. Why had God allowed her husband to be murdered?

The promises and possibilities of a new life sounded so exciting— why had God snatched her dreams away? She wondered if that was really her, that woman so full of joy and hope. She allowed that horrible scene to replay in her mind. Maybe, if she looked at it from a different angle, it would make more sense now. She watched the scene as a spectator.

There was an ugly side of William she had never seen. It couldn't be explained away. Why was he so mean?

When the men rode up to the wagon, William pulled his pistol. That was a mistake. Why did he do that? There were three of them.

He would have had no chance against them in a shootout. The marshal must have felt threatened so he pulled the trigger. Seeing her husband lying in the dust was hard to fathom. She wanted to tell him to get up—to stop playing dead—but she knew that was pointless—he wasn't playing.

Then there was the screaming. It was deafening. It hurt Anne's ears. She wanted to tell the person to stop—but then she realized the sound came from her own throat.

The marshal sat with Anne, trying to calm her, as the deputies wrapped the body in a blanket and draped it over a horse. She watched the deputy carry a shovel—as the captain led the horse to the grave.

All this time the marshal tried to talk to her—to comfort her. The man who killed her dreams must have been insane to think he could help her. How she hated him.

Why was William killed? Anne toyed with a new thought. Was there some dark secret from his past William hid? She dismissed the thought. Impossible! The marshal was obviously a monster, killing an innocent man in cold blood.

That scene continued to play in her mind—over and over. She was locked in those moments and couldn't escape. It was like living in a nightmare there was no waking up from. She desperately wanted the horror to stop.

That night, Anne overheard Logan tell the commanding officer he was leaving for Fort Bridger.

Well, good riddance. Thank You, Lord.

She was glad she wouldn't have to ever see this man again.

An Indian agent arrived at the fort that night. Jeb and the marshal sat with him while Anne kneaded bread dough in the kitchen. She could hear the conversation.

"So, what do you do?" Jeb asked the agent. "It's strange, that in all my years on the prairies, I've never talked with an Indian agent before."

"I am a liaison between the nations and the white folk. It's an important position."

"What do you do?" Logan asked.

"I try to keep the peace between the nations and the white folks. That's getting harder as the whites are encroaching more and more on land they said belonged to the tribes and nations."

"How do you keep the peace?" Jeb asked.

"Well, I keep the government informed about what is happening in the nations. I represent the nations to the government—and the government to the nations."

"How do you know what's happening?" Logan asked.

"I live among the Shoshonne people. I speak their language. My wife is from that nation. I understand their ways. I know who I can trust."

"May I ask an honest question?" Jeb asked.

"By all means."

Jeb continued, "I've heard many Indian agents are corrupt. They mismanage money they have been entrusted with—often spending money that was to help the nations on themselves. Is this true?"

"Sadly, I have heard the same things. I wish it wasn't true. There are good men and corrupt men everywhere. This isn't Heaven yet," the agent said.

"How does one become an Indian agent?" Logan asked.

"Well, some agents were fur traders and became close with the nations. Because they learned the languages and the customs, they were perfect. Sometimes military officers were assigned the position."

"It must be a difficult job," Anne said as she walked out of the kitchen, wiping her hands on her apron.

"It is a difficult job, ma'am. Some Indian agents have tried to take away the leadership roles of the tribal councils and have been found dead."

"That must cause a lot of trouble with the government," Anne said.

"It does. It is understandable the nations don't appreciate an agent overseeing and regulating their lives. I can understand their thoughts."

"It must be difficult for the nations to have to humble themselves to listen to someone they don't know and perhaps don't trust suddenly telling them what they can and can't do," Logan said.

"It's very hard for the nations—especially when they find out their agent cannot be trusted. It's also hard as an agent, because I am expected to report to the government what progress is being made to assimilate these 'pagans' into white society."

"That's pretty arrogant of the government," Anne said.

"Agreed. I am hoping there are enough agents who really care for the nations to make a difference—to protect them from the white man's unjust treatment."

"I hope so too," Logan said.

The agent continued, "Another issue, is some white folk try to get the agents to scheme with them on how to steal from the nations. It can be pretty corrupt—and pretty dangerous for the agents if they don't comply."

"I hope you never run into that. Well, it's been a long night. I'm going to bed. Goodnight," Jeb said.

"Where are you sleeping tonight?" Logan asked.

"Oh, one of the soldiers—I think he said his name is Clayton—said there was a spare room beside his I could use."

"I don't know where my manners have gone. Have you had anything to eat?" Anne asked.

"I haven't eaten since yesterday, ma'am."

"Would you like a loaf of fresh bread?" Anne asked.

"I would be mighty grateful, ma'am."

Anne returned from the kitchen with a loaf of fresh-baked bread, a bowl of butter, and a jug of milk. Her face was flushed from the heat of the stove.

"Thank you, ma'am."

"I apologize for not asking sooner." Anne said.

Walking back to the kitchen, Anne blushed when she heard the men talking.

"She's a mighty fine woman," the agent said.

"I don't think they come any finer," Logan said.

She couldn't help it. Anne turned to look back at Logan. He was gazing at her with a look of adoration on his face. That was strange. Anne quickly looked away.

Back in the kitchen, Anne could still hear the men talking. "She's beautiful, Logan. Is she your wife?"

Logan's reply made her catch her breath. "I wish she was." Did Logan really say that? How dare he? He had no right to say anything like that.

The next morning the marshal rode off.

Good riddance! I hope he never comes back!

But, now Anne had different issues. She was stranded at the fort, with no foreseeable way to leave. Logan was her chaperone. Now that he was gone, was she stranded at Fort Laramie for life? That wasn't her only concern...

Anne slowly sipped a cup of hot milk as she sat by the fire. Grace had offered her a coffee to help her stay awake, but the thought of coffee made her feel ill. Actually, the thought of almost anything to eat or drink made her feel like throwing up. Except apples. She craved apples. She probably ate five of them that day.

I feel completely exhausted. What's wrong with me, Lord?

Anne heard the gentlest voice whisper, "You're having a baby, Anne."

What? A baby? But Lord, how will I care for a baby? I'm all alone. Please be joking...

Just then Anne felt the gentle fluttering of life inside her womb. It felt like butterflies dancing inside her.

Anne didn't know whether to laugh or cry. She was startled at the love she instantly felt for the baby.

She had no idea how God would provide for her and her child. She wanted to trust Him—but things were looking desperate. Being stranded at Fort Laramie with no husband, no way to get to California, no future—and now a baby. It was downright scary.

She wondered why Logan said he wished she was his wife. What a strange thing for him to say. What a horrible man. She could never marry someone like him.

"I'd rather be stranded at this fort for the rest of my life than marry the likes of that man. God, you know I need You. I'm afraid, Lord. I know Your Word says, "When I am afraid, I will trust in You..." [5] but sometimes verses are easy to say—but not as easy to live. Please lead me and help me, Lord."

[5] Psalm 56:3

CHAPTER FOUR

August 1881

Anne's days and nights were a blur. Sunrises and sunsets flew by. Her life seemed to be an endless wheel of eating, sleeping, and working. She wondered if this was really all life was about. She fretted about what was to become of her and her child. How could she continue the horrible hours in the bakery—and nurse and care for a baby? The questions whirled through her mind—causing her so much stress her head ached.

God, what will I do?

God was strangely silent.

The leaves were changing colors when the marshal returned to Fort Laramie. Grace said she heard he was passing through on his way to Fort Hall. Anne was thrilled to hear he would be moving on.

"Howdy, ma'am."

Anne knew the marshal was speaking to her, she could hear joy and excitement in his greeting, but the bitterness in her heart wouldn't allow her to reply.

She should have been with her husband in their home in California by now—not slaving over a hot stove all night every night. It was his fault. She could never forgive him. At least he would be leaving soon. She would just ignore him and soon he would be gone.

The next morning Anne was shocked to see snow. Deep snow. It must have snowed all night. She shivered as she stood warming her hands in front of the fire in the dining room. She hoped Logan would be gone before she would ever have to speak to him.

"Good morning, ma'am," a cheerful voice called out.

She had no intention of ever speaking to that man again, but words seemed to have a mind of their own. "I heard you were leaving..."

"No, ma'am. It would be impossible for a horse to travel far without being worn out in this deep snow."

"So now what will you do?" Anne asked.

"I expect I'll make myself as useful as possible here until the snow melts. Then I'll be on my way. It should be gone in a day or two."

"It won't be any time soon, son."

Jeb had drawn his chair close to the fire. He drew a deep breath on his corncob pipe before he said, "The snow's here to stay, son. May as well unpack your bags and wait till spring."

Spring? Anne couldn't believe the man's words. Was he really staying until spring? No!!

"I've lived in these parts all my life," Jeb continued. "I know when the snow's here to stay."

Jeb tried to get up but seemed to struggle. Logan rushed to his side and helped him up.

Anne turned and walked towards the kitchen. She was completely disgusted by this new turn of events. Logan was staying? Did God want to punish her for hating that man?

"What's the matter with her?" Jeb asked.

"Oh, it's a long story. It doesn't bear repeating."

"Well son, if you're looking for work, I need someone to help me. Life just isn't as easy as it used to be. I have a small cabin out back with two beds. You're welcome to stay with me."

"How can I help you?"

"I could use help drawing water, chopping wood, building fires—that sort of thing. I'll need to build up a supply of wood for the winter. I should have had that done by now but I didn't have the strength. You could help with the animals too."

"I'm sure a good stockpile of wood is necessary for survival," Logan said.

"Yup, a Wyoming winter can be pretty nasty. It gets mighty cold in these parts."

"A bed sounds wonderful. I've been sleeping on my bedroll on the ground for months. The barn is getting mighty cold. I'd be glad to help you until the snow melts, Jeb."

"I can pay you, son."

"There's no need. I'm happy to help you."

Anne could hear the conversation from the kitchen. The marshal spoke so kindly to Jeb. She had a moment of wondering if she had misjudged the man…but then resolutely told herself…

I hate him—he took my William—he ruined my life. I will never forgive him.

Later that evening, Anne sat on the pine bench as she waited for the bread to bake. The delicious smell of baking wafted through the dining room. The warm fire made her feel drowsy. She was just nodding off, her head on the table, when Jeb came in and sat beside her.

"Howdy, Anne."

Anne made herself sit up. "Evening, Jeb."

Jeb smiled as Logan walked into the room. He patted the seat beside him and said to Logan, "Come, sit a spell. I have a story to tell you."

Logan seemed to love Jeb's stories. Anne watched from a dreamy, half-asleep place as Jeb stuffed sweet grass and tobacco into his corncob pipe. He lit it with an ember from the fire, took a deep draw, then continued.

"Before I tell you the story, you have to know this here is one of the most important forts on the Oregon Trail."

"Why's that?" Logan asked.

"It's one of the biggest forts. It was established as a fur-trading fort, to trade with the Indians, but now it's so much more."

"How is it more?" Anne asked in the drowsiest voice Logan had ever heard.

"It's a well-armed military post," Jeb said.

"Do you ever have trouble with the Indians?" Logan asked.

"They're good people. They're fair to trade with and will help a man in a heartbeat."

"But I heard there's been some troubles with the nations around here," Anne said.

"Honestly, the only time there's any trouble is if a white man starts it. But you didn't hear that from me." Jeb winked.

"What do you mean?" Anne asked. She was horrified by the answer.

"Well, for example, I heard some white folk used friendly Indians as target practice."

"What? That's insane. No wonder they started burning wagons," Logan said.

"Yup. The white folk brought it on themselves."

"But why is there no wall around the fort if the Indians aren't happy?" Anne asked.

"I noticed that too," Logan said. "I thought that was kind of strange."

"That's cause there's no need here," Jeb said.

"Why's that?" Logan asked.

"The Indians around here know we mean them no harm. We treat them fair, so there's no need for walls."

"I reckon because this is a well-armed military post, the Northern Plains tribes also realize they'd be foolish to attack," Logan said.

"Yup. You got that right, son. Are you ready for the story?"

"Of course." Logan smiled at Jeb. It was obvious they had a special friendship.

"It was back in 1854 when Lt. Grattan took twenty-nine

soldiers from this fort to a Lakota village. It's just nine miles east. He planned to arrest an Indian a pioneer accused of stealing his cow."

"Is stealing a cow cause for arrest?" Anne sleepily asked.

"Yes, ma'am. Well, the Indian refused to be arrested because he said he hadn't taken the cow. Can't say I blame him for refusing to go with the soldiers if he was innocent."

"If the soldiers weren't fair to the Indians, I can see why he refused to go," Anne said.

"That's right. Well, Lt. Grattan was determined to bring the man back to Fort Laramie. A fight ensued, and the entire US command was wiped out."

"That's a horrid story," Anne said.

"It's a true story, Anne." Jeb paused to puff on his pipe. "Ever since relations have been a bit strained between us and the Indians. Nothing serious now. I believe they're good, decent folk. If we treat them fair, they'll do the same for us."

Jeb continued. He looked at his friends and smiled. "Once Sioux attacked this fort. They were invited back to negotiate terms of peace, but Chief Red Cloud was angry and refused because he heard more army forts were being built on his land. He realized he had been lied to. The land his nation had been promised was being stolen. There really was no chance for peace."

Anne said, "I've noticed the soldiers have rigid routines of daily drills. The officers are very strict."

"That's true. Mild infractions are dealt with severely. Men sometimes disappear as they desert because of the harsh treatment. They take off in the night and brave the elements rather than endure the hardships of military life." Jeb winked, "Don't tell anyone I told you that. It's supposed to be a secret nobody knows about."

Anne wished Clayton would desert…and the marshal would go with him.

"By 1852, over fifty thousand pioneers stopped by this fort. They keep a register in the trading post. Folks stop here as they travel West to California or Oregon—and East if they find the trail too hard and turn back to wherever they came from."

"That's a lot of pioneers," Anne said.

"Folks came to this fort looking for help. There were lots of sick among them. Cholera, scarlet fever, measles, mumps, smallpox, tuberculosis—all diseases common on the trail."

"It sounds like there are many ways for travelers to die," Logan said.

"Yup. There sure are. There's people who starve because they didn't pack enough food, there's disease from dirty water, rattlesnake bites, Indian attacks, thieves, gunshot accidents…"

Ironically, just then a loud gunshot rang out. The blast was so close it made Anne jump. Hot milk spilled all over her dress.

They heard shouting. Several men carried a wounded man into the dining room. Blood covered his chest.

The men lowered the bloodied man onto a table closest to the fire. Another man hollered, "Is there a doctor here?"

No one stepped forward.

"Well, we'll have to help him ourselves."

"What happened?" Jeb asked.

"He was cleaning his gun and it accidentally went off. I think there's lead in his chest."

When the cloth in front of the man's chest was removed, the sight was so gruesome Anne fainted.

Someone asked, "Isn't he the man who stayed in the room next to Clayton?"

"Yup, that's the man."

"Isn't he a government agent? The guy who represents them to the Indians?"

"Yup. That's the man."

"I wonder why he was cleaning Clayton's gun. That's the gun that was lying on the floor next to the man."

The men looked at each other. Now that was a strange question. Why was Clayton's gun in that man's room?

That night, the man died.

CHAPTER FIVE

Logan smiled as he sat down at the table. "Howdy, ma'am. How are you?"

Why did that man have such a beautiful smile? Anne had no intention of telling him about the baby. Why would he care to know?

"I'm okay," Anne said.

"What's on your mind?" Logan smiled. His smiles made it hard to hold a grudge against the man—but she was determined to hate him—for William's sake. Did she dare tell him about the baby? It seemed necessary, as he might be her only possible chaperone to the West.

"I have some surprising news, marshal."

"Oh?"

"I'm having a baby." It was funny he hadn't noticed her bulging belly—but men aren't always aware of the obvious.

"Are you sure? Oh—my apologies. That's a silly question. Of course, you'd know. Are you okay?"

"I'm okay."

Just then, one of the cooks hollered out the kitchen door at Anne. "Missy, if you want to stay here, you'll have to pull your weight. Get in here now."

"What does she want you to do?" Logan asked.

"I have to bake bread. Grace is sick, so they need me to do her work too."

"That's crazy, ma'am. Do they know you are with child? Will you be okay?"

"I'll be fine." Anne said, just before she fainted.

Logan lifted her in his arms and asked directions to her room. He wrapped the bedcovers around her and prayed God would protect her. Then he walked to the kitchen.

"Hi folks. I'm here to report for kitchen duty."

"Where's Anne?"

"She's not feeling well so she's resting. I'm here on her behalf."

The kitchen staff didn't look convinced this was a good idea, but they needed help. One of them said, "Here's your apron and here's a recipe card. Have you baked before?"

"Can't say I have."

"Well, this should be interesting..."

The next morning, the soldiers were surprised to be served very well done, quite crunchy bread. They were asked to pray for Anne, their usual baker—as she was under the weather, and would possibly be for several months. It was announced that Logan—who had never baked before—would do his best to fill in for her. Thankfully, no one complained.

Logan brought Anne bread and soup when he finished his shift. Anne turned her back to Logan when he walked in the room.

"Ma'am, are you okay?" Logan placed the food on the nightstand.

"I'm fine. Thanks for the food, but I'm not hungry."

"I heard a few men say your bread wasn't as good as usual."

Anne turned towards him. "What do you mean?"

"I took your shift and I am proud to say the bread I made was perfect... for target practice."

"Why did you take my shift?"

"You fainted, ma'am. I carried you to your bed."

"I'm obliged, marshal, but I don't require your help. I'm going to help in the kitchen now."

Anne climbed off the bed, and would have fallen to the floor if Logan hadn't caught her. He may have held her a bit longer than was necessary.

"I'm sorry. I have no idea what's wrong with me. I don't know why I'm so tired all the time."

"Maybe it's because you're having a baby? Just rest. I'll take your shifts. I can still help Jeb. I always wanted to learn how to bake."

Logan baked while Anne rested. She knew he was trying to help her, and wondered if it was because he felt guilty for destroying her life.

I still hate him, Lord. But...not as much.

Anne rested all of September. She was determined to get up and get back to work. Walking to the table by the hearth took all her strength. As she sat at the table, trying to work up the strength to be helpful in the kitchen, a cheery voice said, "How's your evening going, ma'am?" The marshal smiled at Anne. She noted his beautiful smile. She wondered how he could be so kind—when she had been nothing but rude to him.

"I'm okay."

"You look exhausted."

"I shouldn't be. I've rested for a month—thanks to you." It was the first time Anne smiled at the marshal. His eyes seemed to sparkle when she smiled. Were those tears in his eyes?

"Ma'am, may I pray for you?"

"I beg your pardon?"

"I just had a strong feeling I need to pray for you."

"Yes. That would be great. Thank you."

The marshal took off his hat and looked out the window at the expansive sky. Anne followed his gaze. Beyond the billions of brilliant stars, the sky looked a deep ink black. The coyotes were singing—asking God for their supper again.

Anne allowed herself to really look at the man who wanted to pray for her. She hadn't noticed before how handsome he was. His face showed integrity, strength, kindness. She had been so busy hating the man she hadn't really seen him. He looked to be about thirty at the most. She admired his sandy-colored hair, his deep blue eyes, the manly look of his face. His tall frame exuded strength. Was God letting her see the marshal as He saw him?

"Dear God, I come to You on behalf of this precious woman…" Anne was startled he called her a precious woman.

"You are the only one who can heal broken hearts and wounded spirits. Lord, please do that for Your beautiful daughter. Amen."

Anne was quiet for so long the marshal finally asked, "Are you okay, ma'am?"

Anne couldn't help herself. She started to cry. "I'm fine. I've never been so fine. When you prayed, I felt God's arms around me—comforting me—holding me. I know He's looking after me and I'll be okay. Thank you for praying, marshal."

"Please call me Logan."

"Thank you, Logan. You can call me Anne."

Later that day, Anne stood in the kitchen, kneading a batch of bread dough, listening to the conversations in the dining room. She was determined to do her share of the work.

Jeb sat by the hearth in the dining room nursing his pipe. She could see he wanted to get every last bit of smoke out of it. Clayton sat with him—with his back to the kitchen. He must have thought no one else could hear, but while Anne mixed the bread dough, she heard every word.

"I can't believe the marshal hasn't told Anne the whole story. He's a fool. Doesn't he see she hates him?"

"What is Logan keeping from her, son?"

"Do you want the whole story?" Clayton asked.

"If you want to tell it…"

"It was in the fall of 1860. The US Army Corps expected the payroll to come in. The laborers at the Muscle Shoals Project on the

Tennessee River looked forward to pay day."

Jeb took a deep draw on his pipe. He looked at the man speaking to him, as if appraising if this man spoke truth.

"Over five thousand dollars was stolen from the Blue Water Camp. The workers still haven't seen their pay. William Ryan, Anne's husband, was part of Jesse James' gang of outlaws."

Anne sucked in a deep breath. He couldn't be serious. Was this possible?

"Jesse and his gang were responsible for the holdup."

What? Was this true? Was William part of a thieving gang?

"Someone was shot during the holdup. The deputy told me the marshal wanted to question William. He was a suspect, but if it wasn't him, the marshal wanted to know if he saw the murderer."

Anne realized if this was true, she had treated the marshal brutally without cause. *Please forgive me, God. Can Logan ever forgive me?*

Jeb took a deep draw on his pipe before he spoke. "How do you know all this, son?"

"My platoon was assigned to find William Ryan. The marshal and his deputy found him first."

The next night, as Logan sat by the hearth by himself, Anne sat down across from him.

"Logan…"

"Yes, Anne."

"I overheard Clayton talking to Jeb."

"And…?"

Anne must have looked faint—she felt sick knowing how she had behaved towards this kind man. The marshal touched her arm and asked, "Are you okay, Anne? Do you need water?"

"I'm fine. Thanks. I heard Clayton say William was part of Jesse James' gang—and was a thief and a murderer. Is that true?"

"Yes."

Anne didn't know if she should scream at him or cry. "Why didn't you tell me?"

Logan looked at Anne with compassion. "Anne, I felt you had

35

enough grief to carry. Knowing about your husband's past would have made your grief even heavier. I wanted to spare you."

"But you knew I hated you. I wished you were dead."

"I know. I saw it in your eyes…your voice…but I couldn't let you be grieved more than you were."

She couldn't believe he was willing to be hated so she wouldn't have more grief.

Who is this man, Lord?

"Oh Logan, I've misjudged you. I'm so sorry. Please forgive me."

Logan looked at her kindly. "There's nothing to forgive, Anne."

She felt a huge weight fall off her shoulders.

"Thank you, Logan."

Anne wandered off to the kitchen. About an hour later she was surprised to see Logan still sitting by the fire in the dining room. He was the only one in the room. The coal oil lantern flickered on the table beside him. The light showed the strength in his face. Anne loved the peaceful scene.

"It's mighty cold." Anne said as she walked to the table. Logan got up and draped a buffalo hide around her.

"I've noticed. Do you need more blankets at night? You could use mine."

"That's very kind, Logan, but I'm fine." Anne got up to go to her room.

"Night, Anne."

"Night, Logan."

As Anne lay on her feather bed, her thoughts were peaceful—the first time since William's death. She wasn't having terrifying thoughts of what would happen to her. She knew God was with her. She knew He would take care of her.

How she had misjudged Logan. That man had been nothing but kind to her—even when she was spitting mad and hating him.

Oh God, please remove all hatred and bitterness from my heart. Thank You for showing me who Logan is—and who William was. I shudder to think what life could have been like with him.

CHAPTER SIX

It was hard to believe so many months passed since Anne arrived at Fort Laramie. The days turned into a familiar routine. Anne thought she could bake bread and Johnny cake now with her eyes closed. She baked in her dreams.

It was a bitterly cold December morning—the kind that makes a person want to stay snug in bed. Anne wondered what Christmas at Fort Laramie would look like. Thankfully, Grace had some wonderful ideas.

Some men were asked to chop down a few evergreens. They were to be set up and decorated in the dining room. It wouldn't be the same for the men as being home, but Grace said it would be special.

Anne was put to work making gingerbread men and stars so they could adorn the trees. That was in addition to the endless loaves of bread she made daily—or nightly—depending on which shift she was on. Apples from the root cellar, strings of popcorn, and a few pieces of candy, would also adorn the trees.

One of the soldiers asked if they could have candles on the trees, but candles were far too precious to use up frivolously. Bees wax was not easy to come by, so Grace said no. Also, candles were a huge fire hazard. They couldn't afford to have the fort turned into a heap of ashes.

Christmas day finally arrived. That day was probably the busiest the fort had ever seen. Everyone had chores. Some tended the animals, while others scrubbed every inch of the fort. While the work was being done, the kitchen hummed with activity. All the women helped that day—all who lived in the fort were going to celebrate the birth of the Christ child together.

Grace and Anne had outdone themselves. They had prepared for weeks. The trees looked beautiful. The smell of cinnamon, cloves, and roasted food wafted in the air. Chestnuts collected in sacks in the fall were toasted in the fire. There were fat turkeys stuffed with sage and wild rice, ham, goose, potatoes mashed with creamy butter, carrots roasted in wild honey, carrot pudding, and there were over twenty huge apple pies with fresh whipped cream waiting on the kitchen counter. Thankfully, Anne hadn't eaten all the apples.

When all was ready, the dinner triangle clanged. The soldiers arrived in the dining room dressed in their finest for Christmas dinner. Their boots had been polished, their brass buttons shone, and even their eyes sparkled with the excitement of young children. After everyone was stuffed, the soldiers took turns entertaining the crowd. Some read poems, one played the bagpipes, some performed hilarious skits, and an officer led the group singing Christmas carols. His rich, baritone voice was louder than the over two hundred voices.

After dinner the soldiers were invited to choose two treats from the trees as a Christmas gift. The gingerbread disappeared in moments.

Clayton sauntered towards Anne, so she quickly disappeared into the kitchen.

Logan moseyed into the kitchen and volunteered to help clean up the dishes. He seemed to be in a hurry. Anne wondered why he was so anxious to help get everything done. Finally, long after the soldiers had gone to bed, Anne was able to sit by the fire with him.

"Anne, I have something for you."

"What is it, Logan?"

"I put it under one of the trees. You'll have to find it."

"But how will I know it's my gift?"

"Oh, you'll know."

Anne hurried to the trees to discover the gift. There were four huge trees. Finally, under the last tree, there was a large something wrapped in a calf skin.

"Is this it, Logan?"

"It is."

Anne squealed with delight then cried when she opened the gift. It was the most beautifully hand-carved cherry wood cradle she had ever seen.

"Logan, it's beautiful! Did you make it?"

"Yes. Do you like it?"

"I love it! It's the most amazing cradle I've ever seen!"

Logan smiled one of his beautiful smiles.

"When did you have time?"

"Well, while Jeb told me stories every night for a couple months, I was able to work on the cradle."

"Logan, how can I ever thank you?"

"It was something God put on my heart. He actually deserves the thanks."

"Thank You, God. But, I don't have anything for you."

"Anne, your happiness is my gift." Logan smiled again.

Anne had to look away. There was a look in his eyes that made her heart leap.

The next night, after a feast of leftovers from Christmas dinner, Jeb entertained all who stayed in the dining room.

"I recall back in 1851—just a few years ago—the government made a treaty with the Cheyenne, the Lakota, and the Arapaho Nations. The US government signed the Treaty of Fort Laramie that promised the Indians if they allowed safe passage of white folks over their lands, the Indians would have sovereignty over the Platte River basin. There was a problem—"

"What was the problem, Jeb?" Clayton rudely interrupted before Jeb could finish the sentence.

"Shut up and let him tell the story," a soldier shouted back at him.

"The gold rush in Colorado made the treaty void, as whites moved onto land that was rightfully the Indians and supposedly protected. This caused huge issues. The Indian land where they lived, hunted, and traded—their ancestral land—was now being overtaken by white folk. The buffalo were being shot for sport. It's sad herds have been wiped out."

Folks sat quietly when Jeb finished. What could they say? There was nothing they could do. They sat deep in thought, then just quietly moved on to their rooms for the night.

Logan waited by the fire. When everyone had left but Anne he said, "Anne, when the weather is mild enough, I plan to head for Oregon. As soon as there's fresh grass for my horse, I'll be on my way."

Surprisingly, a pain stabbed her heart when she thought of Logan leaving. *Lord, what will I do without his support and encouragement? His words—his prayers—they've held me up on days I didn't think I could go on.*

Logan's next words brought her the most joy of all his words.

"Anne, would you like to travel with me to Oregon? I'm inviting Jeb along too."

She thought—*Would I? Oh, my goodness! Yes!* but what she said was, "How would that work with just one wagon?"

"I've already thought it all out. Jeb and I'll sleep in our wagon rolls under the wagon. We'd guard you and take care of the animals and the wagon."

"Oh Logan, I'd love to go! Thank you for inviting me."

"Well, Anne, I couldn't very well leave you here with Clayton."

Anne laughed. It was a joyful laugh. God was in control. He was looking after her and her baby. She put her hand on her tummy and spoke to her little boy. She somehow knew the child was a boy. "God's taking care of us, little man. He hasn't forsaken us. You'll see."

"You can trust God, Anne. He's making a way for you."

But then, an anxious thought flitted across her mind. "Oh— but I have nowhere to go when I get to Oregon."

Logan smiled. His voice brought Anne peace. "Don't worry. God will lead and guide you. Just trust Him."

Why does Logan calm my heart so easily? Thank You, God, for such a good friend.

When Logan went to his room, he could hardly contain his excitement.

"Jeb! Anne said she'd like to travel to Oregon with me!"

"That's mighty fine of you to escort her. Where will she go?"

"I don't rightly know, but I know she can't stay here. I know God will look after her."

"You're a good man, Logan."

"Jeb, I have a question for you."

"Say on, son."

"Who's going to look after you when we leave?"

"Oh, I suspect God will either take me home or bring along another kind soul to help me."

"Jeb, I have a proposal for you."

"I love proposals."

"If you like this idea, Jeb, I'd like to take you with us to Oregon. You have no family. I don't want to leave you here."

Logan was totally unprepared for Jeb's reaction. He burst out crying.

"Son, and you truly feel like my son, I'd be honored to travel with you."

"I don't just mean travel with us, Jeb. I mean I plan to take care of you until Jesus calls you home."

At that Jeb got up, walked with shaky steps to where Logan sat, hugged him, and cried some more.

"That's mighty kind of you, son, but I don't want to be a burden to you."

"Jeb, you could never be a burden. I love you like a father."

"And I love you like a son."

"I can't imagine leaving here without you. Who would tell me stories every night?"

Jeb laughed. "I'd be happy to join you. I'll help as much as I can."

"How do you feel about sleeping on a bedroll under the wagon?"

"No problem. I've been sleeping on bedrolls most of my life. My body's used to that."

"Jeb, I'm glad you are coming with us."

"Me too, son. God has heard the cries of my heart. He does set the solitary in families. [6] You and Anne are my family."

"Jeb, that reminds me of a verse. *The Lord is near to all who call on Him, to all who call on Him in truth. He fulfills the desires of those who fear Him; He hears their cry and saves them.*" [7]

Just then, they heard the piercing screams of a woman. Logan bolted out the door to help. He was horrified when he realized the screams came from Anne.

Anne stood in the middle of her room screaming. Tears streamed down her face. Grace was nowhere to be seen. She must have been on the all-night baking shift. Anne would have been alone in her bedroom. Clayton lay unconscious on the floor. He had a bloody gash across his forehead. Logan stepped over Clayton and rushed to hold Anne in his arms to calm her.

"Anne, whatever happened?"

Anne couldn't speak. She was sobbing and hiccupping hysterically.

"Anne, what happened?"

"He… came…into…my…room. He… lunged at me. He

---

[6] Psalm 68:6
[7] Psalm 145:18-19

tore... my blouse. I grabbed... the water jug... and smashed him... over the head... with it. I didn't mean to kill him."

Clayton started moaning.

"He's not dead, Anne. But if he was no one would blame you."

A group of soldiers appeared at the door. Logan said, "Men, take this man to the commanding officer. He is to be court-martialed and tried for assaulting a lady."

"You haven't seen the last of me, little lady," Clayton hissed at Anne, as he was pulled to his feet and dragged out the door.

"What a horrid man! I can hardly wait to leave this place and get away from him."

"Well, thankfully, that will be soon."

"Today?"

"Not quite that soon—as soon as we see grass for the oxen."

"Tomorrow would be wonderful!"

CHAPTER SEVEN

Independence Rock
March 1882

"Anne, I'm leaving for Fort Bridger tomorrow. It's a Hudson's Bay Company Fort. They've had issues with the Indians and they asked if I could come help calm things down," Logan announced.

"Do you have to leave?" Anne blurted out before she could stop the words. She blushed and suddenly found her shoes very interesting. She wondered how she could be so brash to ask such a question. When she finally looked up, she could see the surprise on Logan's face at her question.

Anne continued, "I'm glad I met you, Logan. I pray God leads and protects you." This was all so strange. Now that she didn't hate him—he was leaving? Was he planning to come back for her?

Logan stood quietly looking at Anne for what seemed like an eternity. Then he smiled as he pulled out a crumpled piece of paper and handed it to Anne.

"Anne, here's the list of what I've packed for our trip."

"Our trip? I'm going with you?"

"Yup. Jeb's finishing up with the last of the supplies. You only have to bundle up your clothes and we'll be ready to leave first thing in the morning."

Anne's heart was racing with excitement as she read the list out loud.

"60 pounds of hardtack (fried flour, water, sugar, and salt)
300 pounds of flour
200 pounds of bacon
30 pounds of coffee
20 pounds of tea
50 pounds of sugar
100 pounds of lard
dried apples
200 pounds of rice
200 pounds of beans
A sack of cornmeal (hopefully Anne doesn't decide to wear it…)"

Anne laughed. "Logan, I don't plan to wear any of the supplies."

"I couldn't resist writing that, Anne."

"Will this be enough for two to three months?" Anne asked.

"That's exactly half of what's called for a trek from Missouri to Oregon. I packed the eggs in cornmeal and the bacon's packed in bran. There's still some food in your wagon, but now there's more than enough to share with others in need."

"That sounds good, Logan. Thank you for taking care of the supplies. What do I owe you?"

"You're providing the wagon and the oxen. You don't owe me anything."

"I feel like my favorite words to you are thank you."

"You're welcome. Did I forget anything you'd like?"

"Umm…yes! Molasses so I can make you gingerbread cookies. I've noticed you like them."

Logan grinned, "Yours are the best."

Anne was so excited she wouldn't be baking for over two hundred people. They would be like a little family. The Johnny cake and cornmeal mush would be so easy to make. She had all the ingredients for soda biscuits and bread.

"Thank you again, Logan."

Logan just smiled, the most beautiful smile she had ever seen. "Come, let me show you the wagon."

A large barrel of water was attached to the side of the wagon. They would have to boil all water for drinking and cooking to kill off bacteria that could cause disease. They knew cholera was common on the trail. Jeb told them most deaths from disease happened west of Fort Laramie. That's the way they were headed.

Thankfully they had a sturdy wagon. William made sure he bought the best prairie schooner money could buy. He bought the best of everything. Anne shuddered as she thought of where the money came from. To outfit a wagon normally cost about one thousand dollars—four hundred for the wagon and the rest for supplies.

Logan offered to carry Anne's bundle of clothes into the wagon. She followed him and was surprised to see a new feather 'tick' on the rope bed.

"Logan, did you make this?" Anne couldn't help herself. She dropped herself onto the quilt and was immediately wrapped in soft folds.

"I did. I made it so you and the baby would be comfortable."

Anne couldn't make herself get up. The bed was too comfortable. A voice came from within the folds of the blanket. "Thank you, Logan. It's wonderful. It's what I'd imagine lying on a cloud would feel like."

"I filled that cloth sack with wool and feathers. I hoped you'd like it," Logan said.

The voice spoke from even deeper in the blanket. "I love it! Thank you again!"

There were a few other folks who had been trapped by the early snow, so they planned to travel together—all three wagons. That wasn't nearly enough for safety. Usually up to one hundred wagons travelled together. They really had no other options. The folks at the fort had been kind enough to let them stay for the winter—but it was time to move on.

"A scout said there's a huge train approaching. As soon as it leaves, we can leave with it." Logan said.

"What if Clayton escapes and decides to desert and join that train?" Anne asked.

"He won't escape from the jail, and if he did he wouldn't join a wagon train. There'd be wanted posters out in every town for him. He's a man completely without morals or integrity, but he's not a fool."

The next morning, there was no sign of the wagon train so Logan said they would wait. The huge wagon train didn't show up all that week. They got word folks on that train were too sick to travel. Jeb, the Wilsons, the Morgans, Anne and Logan prepared to leave the next morning.

The next morning, Anne was surprised to see Cheyenne and Sioux hunters camped outside the American Fur Trading Company. They had mounds of buffalo hides their women had painstakingly cured. The men waited patiently for the store to open so they could trade their furs for things they needed.

Several Indians already had their courage bolstered by the white man's firewater. A few brave Indians came into the fort. One man saw Anne and announced to all he would like to buy the squaw. He looked around to see who he should bargain with. Seeing Logan, he swaggered over to him and said, "I buy woman."

Logan looked surprised. "What woman?"

"This woman." The man smiled a toothless smile as he pointed at Anne.

Anne was annoyed that Logan looked amused.

"Oh, my friend, she is a very valuable squaw. She carries a child within."

The Indian gasped. "A child? I no want woman with child." He turned and slowly staggered out the door.

"Logan, that wasn't funny."

"But Anne, I was making him aware that he didn't really want you. It worked. But he's crazy not to have made an offer anyway.

Anyone would want you—even with a child."

"Logan…"

"Well, it's true."

That man. Why does he smile at me like that?

The ride from Fort Laramie to Independence Rock was the bumpiest Anne could recall. For one hundred and eighty miles— eighteen days of travel—the ride was so uncomfortable Anne walked most of the way. The good thing about the bumps was if you hung a pail of milk under the wagon, by the end of the day you had delicious, creamy butter.

They were only travelling about ten miles a day. Anne wondered if this was going to take forever to get to Oregon City.

One night, as they sat around the campfire, close to the Sweetwater River, the folks gathered to hear Jeb tell a story.

"Fort Laramie's also called Fort Sacrifice, cause that's where so many folks realize they have too many provisions so they have to discard some. Why, I once saw a piano on the side of the trail. I betcha someone cried when it had to be abandoned."

"I've seen so much left behind too, Jeb," Mrs. Wilson said. "Books, furniture, wagon parts…so much stuff."

"Not too far from here is Independence Rock," Jeb continued. "Thousands of pioneers carved their names in that rock. It's made of granite and is one hundred and twenty-eight feet high. It's called the register of the desert."

That night, as the wind whipped fire sparks around the weary travelers, Logan asked, "Are you warm enough, Anne?"

"Thanks for asking, Logan. I don't know why but I do feel chilled." Logan placed a beautiful Indian blanket around her. "Take this with you in the wagon."

"But, Logan. That's your only blanket besides your bedroll."

"I'll be fine. I want to be sure you and the baby are comfortable."

Anne felt a rush of warmth in her heart towards this man.

Lord, thank You for sending such a kind friend.

At that moment, Anne was surprised to hear Mrs. Wilson

announce she would like to be the breakfast cook.

"Are y'all okay with that? If I'm cooking for two, I can surely just add a bit more and cook for seven."

The faces reflected in the light of the fire looked surprised then joyful. A cheer went up from the group. That's when Mrs. Morgan spoke up.

"I'd like to be in charge of dinners. That would give Anne more time to rest. All in favor?"

All voices cheered again. It was very obvious now Anne was with child. The little group felt like family. No one wanted to go to bed, but they knew 4:00 a.m. would come mighty early, so they said good night and wearily headed off to bed.

Around noon the next day Jeb called out, "There's Independence Rock." He pointed at a huge granite slab. "Lots of folks carve their names into the rock to show others they travelled this way."

Logan smiled at Anne. "Would you like to carve your name in the rock?"

"I would love to."

The rock looked even more imposing up close. It rose straight into the air from the prairie floor, inexplicably placed in the middle of the flattest land you ever saw.

"It's hard to carve," Anne said as she tried to scrawl 'Anne' on the granite wall.

"Here, let me help you."

"Why did you write, Logan and Anne?"

"Well, we're traveling together, so it seemed right." Anne noticed—again—how Logan's blue eyes twinkled when he smiled.

"Are you going to write Jeb's name with ours? He's with us too."

"Unfortunately, there's a piece of rock jutting out right at the end of your name so Jeb's name doesn't fit."

"Convenient."

"Very."

"We're headed to Devil's Gate tomorrow. It's only a day

away."

"What a horrid name. It makes me shudder."

"I know. It's crazy what names some folks come up with."

"Logan, do you ever have a feeling that something is about to happen—almost like God is warning you—telling you to prepare?"

"Sometimes. Why?"

"Cause that's how I feel about Devil's Gate."

CHAPTER EIGHT

Devil's Gate, Wyoming
April 1882

The next morning, as they sat at breakfast, Jeb told Mrs. Wilson, "If you don't start bacon in a cold pan, the outside will crisp up, but raw fat will be trapped inside the bacon."

"I'm pretty sure I know how to cook bacon," Mrs. Wilson snapped.

Anne couldn't help ask, "How do you know so much, Jeb?"

"Well, Anne, when you've lived as long as I have, you pick up a lifetime of information along the way."

That was the first time Anne really looked at Jeb. He appeared to be past seventy years. His face was weathered from the sun, his hands gnarled, and his grey eyes twinkled with kindness.

I've listened to a lot of his stories, but I don't really know much about this man.

"Jeb, where are you from?"

"I'm from so many places I don't rightly know where to say I'm from."

"What did you do for work?"

"I herded cattle on ranches all my adult life."

"Did you ever marry?"

"I wasn't the marrying kind. Just couldn't see myself stuck in one place. I had a wandering spirit."

"How did you end up at Fort Laramie?"

"I just blew in one day like a ball of tumbleweed—and ended up staying a few years. I helped with the animals. Lately, though, I've been getting mighty tired. I wasn't sure how long they would allow me stay if I couldn't keep up my end of the work. It's a blessing Logan invited me along."

"We're glad to have you," Logan said as he munched on a chewy piece of bacon.

That night, as she looked up at the heavens, Anne sighed and said, "Our times are in Your hands." She didn't realize she spoke aloud until Logan asked, "What did you say, Anne?

"Oh nothing much. Just thinking out loud…"

They huddled close to the fire as there was a chill in the air. Anne gazed at the huge expanse of stars. Logan followed her gaze.

"What were you thinking?" Logan asked.

"So many things…like how the Heavens really do declare the glory of God[8]…and how our lives can change in a heartbeat."

"Do you mean what just happened?" Logan asked.

"Yes—but even more than what just happened."

"What do you mean?"

"Well, if I hadn't answered a gentleman's ad, I never would have become a mail-order-bride. If I hadn't become a mail-order bride, I wouldn't be sitting here."

"That seems to be a common way for folks to meet nowadays."

"A few of my friends met their husbands that way," Anne said.

"I wouldn't want a mail-order bride. I'd want to know and love the woman I was going to spend my life with." Logan smiled at Anne. She had to look away.

"Meeting William in Independence, Missouri, the day we

---

[8] Psalm 19:1

married, didn't seem strange at all. He was over twenty years older but that didn't matter."

"Did you know he was so much older when you agreed to marry him?"

"We had written a few letters, but age was never mentioned. After we married, he told me he was forty something."

"You look about nineteen."

"I am. I cared more about the character of the man than his age. From his messages, William seemed to be a good man. I did find it a bit odd he never spoke about his past. Ever."

Logan looked thoughtful. "Maybe he honestly wanted a different life."

"His letters said he planned to buy land, homestead, settle down, start a new life. There were only four letters. He had a dream. It was my dream too. He spoke about a longing for home—a place to belong. That spoke to my heart. I feel like I have been longing for home all my life."

"Anne, I imagine he had a terribly hard life. I'm sure he must have wanted something different."

"It makes me think of a Bible verse. *God isn't mocked. Whatever a man sows, this will he also reap*,"[9] Anne said.

"That man's widow was left to fend for herself with seven children."

"I shouldn't complain."

What a horrible thought. William left another man's wife a widow.

"May I pray for you?"

Anne was snapped out of her reverie by Logan's question. "Why?"

"It's on my heart to pray for you."

"Yes. Thank you."

Logan took off his hat and looked up into the masses of stars.

"Dear God, please look after Anne. She needs You."

---

[9] Galatians 6:7

"That's it?"

"That's what is on my heart."

The next day, they passed a deep gorge carved in the Rattlesnake Mountains by the Sweetwater River. It was breathtakingly beautiful, but an extremely treacherous part of the journey. Anne often held her breath as they navigated the winding, narrow road. She was grateful when they finally paused for the noon meal. It was a reprieve from the frightening trail.

While they ate the rabbit stew Mrs. Morgan made the night before, Anne started having horrific abdominal pains. *What's happening, Lord?*

She excused herself saying she needed to find a bush, but as soon as she stood there was an explosion of blood and water between her legs. The world turned black with tiny stars flashing before her eyes as Anne crumpled to the ground. Logan rushed to her side.

"Anne! Anne! Dear God, don't let Anne die!"

"Is there anything I can do?" Mrs. Morgan asked.

"Maybe she should have a blanket. I think she might be in shock."

Mrs. Morgan ran to the wagon to retrieve a blanket. Anne started moaning. The pain seemed to be coming in waves. The men stood by helplessly.

"Jeb, call Mrs. Wilson! She went to her wagon. Hurry!"

In a few heartbeats Mrs. Wilson kneeled beside Anne.

"What's wrong with her?" Logan asked anxiously.

Mrs. Wilson said sadly. "It's too soon for the child to be born."

Mercifully, Anne remained unconscious throughout the birth. Afterwards, Logan carried Anne to the wagon and gently laid her on the feather bed. He covered her in his blanket. Then he went to look after the baby. He cried as he gently wrapped the dead child in a blanket and walked off to bury him.

The next morning Logan had coffee and cornmeal mush ready for Anne before she even woke up. He paced anxiously outside her wagon, carrying the breakfast, waiting for a sleepy blonde head to appear. When it did, Logan said, "Don't climb down. You need to rest, Anne. We aren't moving today. Here's breakfast for you."

Anne looked at this kind, handsome man gratefully. God had been so gracious to give her such a strong protector. What would happen when they got to the end of the trail and they had to say goodbye? She didn't want to think about that now. Just one day at a time.

"What happened, Logan?"

"I'm sorry to tell you this. Your baby came too soon and is dead."

Anne wailed. "No! No, God! Why?"

Without even thinking if this was the proper thing to do, he couldn't help himself, Logan climbed up into the wagon and took Anne in his arms. He rocked her gently and murmured in her ear, "Shhh. It's okay, Anne. Your baby is with Jesus now. He's safe."

Anne whimpered then quieted down. The arms holding her felt so strong and comforting.

"Do you have a name for your son?"

"A son! I had a son? I thought he was a boy! I want to see him."

"I'm afraid that's impossible. I already buried him."

Anne pulled away from the strong arms and demanded, "Why didn't you let me see my son?"

"I'm sorry, Anne. He was dead inside your body for a while. Mrs. Wilson said it was best if you didn't see him."

"You should have let me make that decision." Anne felt twinges of the old hatred towards this man.

"Anne, please trust me. It would have been very hard for you. Mrs. Wilson's right. This is best."

"But I want to see my baby." Anne burst out crying again.

"I understand. What's his name? I'll write it on the cross over his grave."

"Josiah."

"That's a good name."

"I picked that name months ago. It means, God supports and heals."

"Anne, God is supporting and healing you. You'll see Josiah one day—and he will be perfect—with no spot or blemish."

"I'd like to see his grave."

Logan gently lifted Anne in his arms then climbed down with her from the wagon.

As they stood beside Josiah's grave, Logan asked, "May I pray with you, Anne?"

"Please…"

Logan put his arms around Anne to comfort her while he prayed. Suddenly it was very difficult for Anne to concentrate. Logan's arms were too distracting—and his smell—he had the heady scent of sage and wild honey.

"Dear God, thank You for Josiah's life. Thank You that You saw him before he was even created in his mother's womb. Thank You that he is fearfully and wonderfully made. Thank You, Lord God, this precious child is safe in Your arms. Please give Anne peace, comfort her heart, strengthen her, and help her heal. Amen."

"Thank you."

Anne had never felt so cared for…

"I pray you will be okay, Anne."

"The cross looks beautiful, Logan."

That night there were fierce winds and torrential rains. The winds howled across the prairie. It was the most spectacular lightning storm Anne had ever seen. She wondered if the canvas was going to be torn off the wagon. The whole contraption groaned as if it was dying. Logan and Jeb came to the wagon door with pleading looks on their faces. "Please ma'am, may we come in out of the rain?" They looked so pathetic Anne had to laugh.

"Of course."

The men gratefully climbed into the shelter of the wagon.

"Thank you, Anne."

The men wrapped themselves in their bedrolls and curled up on the wagon floor. The wind howled the entire night. The best part of the storm was the mosquitoes and black flies were blown away.

They awoke the next morning to a brilliantly sunny day. It was as if the storm had been a nasty dream.

Logan knew crossing the ridge of the Rocky Mountains without hurting Anne was going to be difficult. He led the oxen at as slow a pace as possible. Anne tried to walk, but it was impossible. As she lay on the feather bed, the jarring of the wagon made her want to cry out—but she made herself be quiet so as not to alarm Logan.

The nightmare trek seemed to go on forever. Anne quoted a favorite Bible verse over and over until her heart felt at peace. *"For this light momentary affliction is preparing for us an eternal weight of glory beyond all comparison."*[10] She loved that verse. It had carried her through many dark, dreary days.

They travelled slowly that day, cautiously going over the steep mountain passes. They were conscious that even if the travel was slow, each mile brought them closer to Oregon. The views were spectacular. Lush green valleys surrounded by majestic, snow-topped mountains. The higher elevations had thick groves of fir. It was a glorious land!

Stopping for the night, Anne helped Mrs. Duncan prepare the evening meal. All food was shared in common. It reminded Anne of the second chapter of Acts.

"And all that believed were together, and had all things common; And sold their possessions and goods, and parted them to all men, as every man had need. And they, continuing daily with one accord in the temple, and breaking bread from house to house, did eat their meat with gladness and singleness of heart, Praising God, and having favour with all the people..."[11]

Anne had always loved those verses and wondered what it would be like to have such brotherly love. Now she experienced it—and it was beyond anything she could ever have imagined.

---

[10] 2 Corinthians 4:17
[11] Acts 2:44-47

CHAPTER NINE

Fort Bridger, Wyoming
April 1882

Just as they finished their supper of boiled potatoes and dried fish, the group was surprised to see a lone wagon heading east. The wagon halted a distance from their camp. "Stay away!" a voice called out.

"Why?" Mr. Morgan called back.

"Cholera. There were thirty wagons. I'm the only one left. I'm heading back."

"Any idea how it hit your wagon train so hard?"

"I'm pretty sure the water's full of cholera. Dead animals floating in it. Don't drink from the lake up ahead."

"Is there anything we can do for you? Do you need anything?"

"If you have some extra cornmeal, I'd be much obliged."

Jeb carried a sack of cornmeal to the wagon.

"Thank you, friend," the man called out. "I best be movin' on." The man slapped the reins on his oxen and continued down the trail. It was one of the loneliest things Anne had ever seen.

God, please be with that man. It's going to be mighty hard for him to survive on his own. Please protect him, Lord. Thank You that You've kept us safe.

The water they came across ran swiftly. Jeb said that wasn't the water the man warned them about. Cholera couldn't be in fast moving water. Even so, some wouldn't touch it—even after it was boiled. Jeb insisted it was fine. He told everyone it had a sweet taste—pure and clear—the best water he ever tasted. Even so—no one trusted the water.

Two days later Jeb was deathly sick. He had a fever and chills.

"Is he going to be okay, Logan?"

"I don't know. Is all I can do is keep spooning water in his mouth, and hope and pray for the best."

Dear Lord, please don't let Jeb die. Please, Lord.

The next morning, the men buried Jeb.

Lord, you didn't answer my prayer. Why? Jeb was a good man. He was like a father to Logan and me. Why, Lord?

Silence.

Lord, I know You are good. I know You are faithful. Even when I don't understand Your ways, even when I don't see why, I know I can trust You. But I have to tell You, today it's mighty hard to trust You.

Anne waited. Would God speak to her heart? Silence.

Thankfully, Lord, cholera isn't infectious. It's only spread by drinking something polluted by bacteria. Lord, please keep our little group safe.

"We should be in Fort Bridger tomorrow," Logan said. "If you aren't feeling well enough to travel, because it only gets rougher from here, we can stay at the fort until you feel better. I'll need to help settle things with the Indians—and I'm not sure how long that will take. We could join up with another wagon train later."

The thought of abandoning their little family sounded worse than the rigors of the trail. Anne couldn't imagine leaving Mrs. Wilson or Mrs. Duncan. She didn't realize that was exactly what she might have to do.

It was a perfect moonlit night. The wagons were pulled as close to the fire as possible. The Wilsons and the Morgans had retired for the night. Anne looked across the fire at Logan with a heart full of questions.

"Logan, why didn't Hoss come with us?"

"Do you mean my deputy?"

"Yes."

"Well, he got homesick for Independence. He has some family back there. I guess the thought of being totally on his own was too much for him."

"What happened?"

"I relieved him of his duties. He said he will wait at Fort Laramie for a wagon train heading east."

"It's funny, he reminded me of my father—a shadow that rarely spoke. I didn't even realize he wasn't here until now," Anne said. "May I ask you some questions?"

"Sure."

"Why did you become a marshal?"

"Well, to be honest, it didn't top the list of what I wanted to do with my life."

"And that was…?"

"I wanted to be a rancher. I guess I missed my chance."

"Why's that?"

"My Ma and Pa died without leaving a will. My oldest brother decided the ranch was his. I didn't argue."

"So, some of the land was yours?"

"It was, but it wasn't worth fighting over. I've discovered life is uncertain. Plans, hopes, and dreams can be dashed in a moment."

"Yes, I know."

"I'm sorry, Anne. I wasn't meaning to remind you."

"It's okay. I just wanted you to know I understand."

"So, Anne, I find in life we make choices—without really knowing what the consequences of those choices will be."

"And what consequences of your choices has your life brought you?"

"A lot of pain, Anne. I'm not the killing kind of man. I grieve over the death of people. I don't know if my job is sending men into a godless eternity."

"So, this isn't what you anticipated your life would be like?"

"Not at all. I wanted a ranch, a wife, children, a home. I feel like that's all been snatched from me. That's another consequence of my choice."

"Why can't you have a wife, children, and a home?"

"That's not fair to a woman, Anne. A lawman's life is uncertain. I could be shot at any moment. The stress on a woman with a husband like that would be unbearable. I could never marry."

"Logan, I see where circumstances got in the way of your plans. I believe God is bigger than all that. He wants to give us the desires of our hearts if we love and trust Him."[12]

"I trust God, Anne, but I struggle to believe my dreams are His dreams for me. So, I'm determined to follow Him as a single man all the days of my life."

Anne's heart ached when she thought of that dear man going through life alone. His brother took all the money—but there was no bitterness in Logan's voice when he told her that. He was just relaying a fact. He was a very special man.

The next morning, getting the wagon ready to move seemed strange without Jeb's help. He had always been there to give a willing hand or a helpful idea.

Lord, I miss that man, Anne thought.

As the oxen plodded down the trail, Anne admired the bright green poplar's baby leaves fluttering in the breeze. Spring was Anne's favorite time of year.

She couldn't help but think she would have been in California by now if Marshal Logan hadn't appeared. She felt a twinge of bitterness. If only he hadn't arrived. How did Logan know for sure her husband was a murderer? Maybe it was all a tragic mistake? Maybe Logan murdered the wrong man? Somehow, the hatred started creeping back into her heart. It seemed to be sapping the life out of her but she couldn't stop it. *I hate this resentment that keeps*

[12] Psalm 37:4

cropping up. Please Lord, change my heart.

They arrived at Fort Bridger late that afternoon. Anne hadn't realized how exhausted she was until she saw the gates of the fort. Somehow, the weariness of the trail crept up on her.

"Anne, are you okay?"

Logan noticed Anne's face turn deathly pale. Before she could even answer, she fainted into his arms.

Logan lifted her and carried her into the fort. A very matronly Mrs. Duncan took one look at Anne and said, "There's a room down the hall with a good bed. First door on your right. She's welcome to it. The name's Mrs. Duncan. Call me if you need anything."

Logan carried Anne to the room. By this time, she was delirious.

Logan hurried down the hall and called, "Mrs. Duncan, may I have a jug of water and a cloth? Anne has a fever."

"What's wrong with her?" Mrs. Duncan asked as she poured cool water into a bowl.

"I think she's emotionally and physically exhausted. So much has happened to her in the last few months. Her husband was killed. Her baby was born too soon to live. A good friend of hers, someone she loved like a father, died of cholera and was buried on the trail. I think it's all been too much for her."

"Did she lose a lot of blood when she lost her baby?"

"Yes. Why do you ask?"

"She needs time to rest. If I were you, if you want this woman to live, you'll stay put until there's roses in those cheeks."

Logan carried the jug of water to the room, and gently wiped Anne's face with cool water. "Well, Anne, it looks like we're going to be spending some time at Fort Bridger."

Anne moaned slightly. Logan touched the cool cloth to her lips.

"Dear Lord, please protect Anne. Please keep her safe. Thank You, Lord."

Logan gently moved a lock of golden blonde hair off Anne's face.

"Lord, You sure created a beautiful, precious woman. But she's *kind of frail. She needs Your strength, Lord.*"

Days later, Anne was startled to wake up in a strange room, tucked in a bed with a massive goose feather comforter on top of her. She was surprised to see Logan sitting in a chair beside the bed. As soon as she opened her eyes, Logan leaped to her side and held her hands.

"Anne, you're awake…"

"Where am I, Logan?"

"Fort Bridger. You've been sleeping for days. Mrs. Wilson and Mrs. Morgan would like to see you. May I get them?"

"Of course."

The folks traveling on the little wagon train waited to see if there was any improvement with Anne. There wasn't. She barely had the strength to get out of bed. Mrs. Wilson and Mrs. Morgan sat by Anne's side and cried softly as they said goodbye.

"We're sorry, Anne. We wish we could stay until you're better, but we need to move on."

Anne said, "I understand. I'm sorry to see you go. I pray we meet up this side of eternity one day."

Anne tried to sit up to hug them goodbye, but didn't have the strength. The women took turns leaning over Anne to kiss her cheek.

"Goodbye, dear Anne. We love you."

They all cried.

When they left Logan said, "I'm sorry Anne. I know you'll miss them, but this is for the best. If you were to travel now, I don't think you'd make it. I pray you get better soon. I bought you some quills, ink, and a small notebook—so you can write your thoughts about life while you recuperate. I found the diary and pens at the Mercantile."

"Thank you, Logan. That was very thoughtful of you."

"Well, I need to be going."

Then Logan did something surprising. He bent over the bed and kissed Anne on the forehead. Anne blushed.

"Well, now I know how to get some color in those cheeks,"

Logan laughed.

Anne smiled. "Thank you again, Logan."

Logan squeezed Anne's hands. "I'm helping calm the Indian uprising—but I had to make sure you're okay first."

"I'm okay."

"I hope you have a good afternoon, Anne. I'll see you soon."

Logan hesitated at the door. He looked like he had no desire to leave. Anne smiled at him as he left the room. *Such a handsome man. It's a pity he will never marry. He would make someone a fine husband.*

67

CHAPTER TEN

Salt River Range, Wyoming
May 1882

Anne ran her fingers over the smooth leather cover on the journal. It must have cost Logan a lot of money. Notebooks were rare. Why would he buy her such an extravagant gift? She chewed on the end of the pen, wondering what to write.

Dear Diary,

I've never had a diary before, so I don't exactly know what to say. Logan gave me this journal to write my thoughts about life. He is such a kind, thoughtful man.

So, first of all, I want to thank You, God, for looking after me—all the days of my life. From the moment my eyes first opened on Earth, You were there. Actually, You've always been there. Before I was even conceived You knew me. How amazing is that? When my eyes close for the last time on Earth, I know You will be there, too.

Thank You that You gave me a precious baby boy—that you fashioned His little body—forming it from almost nothingness. I stand in awe of Your creation. I am so thankful Josiah is with You now. He has been spared the trials of this life.

I am thankful that one day I will see my little man—thankful he is in Your loving care. Thank You for the privilege to carry this little one for almost seven months. I don't know why he had to go to Heaven now, but You know. Would he have followed in his father's footsteps? You spared him all the evil of this life. Josiah was a special gift, created by your loving hand. He is Yours.

Thank You, Lord, for Logan. What a dear friend. I have never met a kinder man. Please keep Him in Your care. I imagine being a marshal can be pretty dangerous at times. Please protect him. Thank You, Lord.

When Logan walked into the room later that afternoon, Anne was sleeping peacefully. The journal was still in her hand. He stood for a moment, not wanting to disturb her, wanting more time just to look at her. She had such a sweet expression on her face.

Finally, Logan smiled at Anne and said, "Hey, sleepy head."

"Oh…I must have fallen asleep. The last thing I remember was writing in the journal."

"What did you write?"

"Would you like to see it?"

"I'd love to, if it's not personal."

Anne watched Logan as he read the notes.

He's so handsome, Lord—so kind—so thoughtful. Thank You for such a special friend.

"This is wonderful, Anne. I'm glad you're no longer dwelling on how much you hate me and hoping I will die."

"Oh, you silly man. Why would I dwell on that nonsense?"

"Don't act all innocent with me, little missy. I saw that in your eyes for months."

"I'm sorry, Logan. Forgive me for being so stupid."

"Well, I'll have to think about that…"

"Have you thought about it yet?"

"Yes. You are forgiven."

"Thank you."

"So, are you getting up for dinner? There's a seat by the

fireplace for you."

"It's dinnertime already?" Anne asked.

"It is. Mrs. Duncan made a shepherd's pie because I told her it's your favorite. She said something about it would help you get stronger. She'll be thrilled to see you."

As they slowly walked down the hallway to the dining room, Logan kept his arm around Anne. He said it was to support her. Anne pretended to require more support than she really needed.

Logan grinned as he looked at Mrs. Duncan. "Here she is!" he announced.

"Well, just look who the cat dragged in," Mrs. Duncan laughed. Anne smiled at her as she sank into a chair.

The room had a heavenly scent. Had food ever smelled so good? Mrs. Duncan was a fabulous cook. It was obvious she loved food way too much.

After dinner, as Anne sat by the fire, Logan draped a blanket around her.

Anne laughed. "You can stop treating me like a baby. I'm getting better."

After dinner, Logan asked if Anne would like a short tour of the fort.

"Thank you, Logan. I'd love to see Fort Bridger."

"By the way, Anne. I heard that Jesse James was recently shot and killed. I think he was the last survivor of his gang."

"It's sad to think where those evil men are now, Logan, unless they repented before they stepped into eternity."

Logan wrapped her in a buffalo hide then put his arm around her—to brace her so she wouldn't fall he said—and escorted her down a rickety wooden walkway. Fort Bridger was a lot smaller than Anne imagined it would be—not nearly the size of Fort Laramie.

"Here's the trading post... and a blacksmith shop... and a couple small homes with sod roofs." You're staying in the one Mr. Bridger built back in about 1843. I'm staying in the barn."

"That doesn't seem fair. Why do you always get the barn?"

"It's fine. It's warm and dry."

"What's the fort used for?"

"It's a fur-trading post—and a place where pioneers stop to replenish supplies."

"I see."

"This is where the trail goes North to Oregon or South to California. Which way do you want to go, Anne?"

"I was heading for California, but now I'm not sure if that's where God wants me."

"I'm heading to Oregon. If you'd like a chaperone, your destination is Oregon."

"Well then, Oregon it is."

Logan smiled as he escorted Anne back to sit by the fire.

"Are you feeling like you could travel, Anne?"

"I think so…"

"I'd like to head out soon. I figure it will take about ten days just to get to the Salt River Range. Then it's at least another ten days to Soda Springs."

"Soda Springs is a lovely name," Anne said.

"It's a lovely place to rest for a day. If we make good time Fort Hall is five days past Soda Springs."

"I think I'm up to that. Thank you for giving me time to rest."

"Let me walk you back to your room."

Logan gave Anne a hug. "Goodnight, Anne."

Anne lay on the bed that night, thinking about all that had recently transpired.

Lord, why does it seem like Logan had to tear himself away from me—as if he wanted to hold on and never let me go? I don't understand the man. He doesn't want a wife—yet, he told Jeb he wished I were his wife. Are all men so confusing?

Thank You, Lord, I will see Jeb one day. Thank You for that dear man.

I'm grateful little Josiah is with You. His body is lying on the side of the Oregon trail—but, I know he's safely wrapped in Your love in Heaven. Thank You for preparing my heart, knowing something was going to happen. You turned Devil's Gate into Heaven's Gate for my little man. Thank You that You've given me assurance I will see my son again."

The next morning a chilly downpour dampened Anne's thoughts of heading for Oregon.

Surely Logan won't want to travel today.

Anne walked into the kitchen. It was her first time in days she was able to move without help. Mrs. Duncan was busy making biscuits.

"Well, my dear, how was your visit with Logan last night?"

Anne wondered how she knew anything about their walk around the fort.

"It was nice. Logan said we need to be moving on soon."

"He's a mighty fine man, Anne."

"I know that, Mrs. Duncan."

"I'm not sure if I should tell you this…"

Mrs. Duncan took a deep breath and then paused. "Lord, give me wisdom."

Mrs. Duncan waited so long to speak again Anne finally asked, "What do you need wisdom for, Mrs. Duncan?"

"I'm trying to decide if I should tell you this or not."

There was another long pause. Finally, Mrs. Duncan blurted, "Do you realize Logan is in love with you, my dear?"

"What? That's not possible…"

"It's true. I see it in his eyes every time he looks at you. It's in his voice when he says your name."

"Mrs. Duncan, I am sure you're imagining things. He said he can never marry…"

"You'll see, Missy. Just wait…"

The rain cleared and the morning was the sunniest morning Anne had ever seen. The dew sparkled on the grass. Meadowlarks sang. All creation seemed to glow—and Mrs. Duncan thought Logan loved her. Why was her heart singing at the thought? As she sat at the breakfast table, Logan reached for her hand and asked, "Anne, are you up to traveling?"

"Yes, but, there aren't any wagon trains here yet to travel with."

"We'll be fine. Trust God, Anne."

As they were about to pull out of the gate, Anne was surprised to see two women jumping up and down, waving frantically and shouting, "Surprise!"

Was it really Mrs. Wilson and Mrs. Morgan? They hadn't left without her after all?

"Well, Anne girl. We couldn't very well leave you to do all the cooking by yourself," Mrs. Morgan laughed.

Anne cried. "Mrs. Wilson and Mrs. Morgan, you must be the dearest women ever."

Mrs. Wilson beamed as she spoke. "Oh, hush now. That's enough of that sort of talk. We decided we'd wait for you to get better—no matter how long it took."

Anne turned to Logan.

"Did you know about this?"

Logan tried unsuccessfully to look innocent. He laughed and said, "Well, maybe I had a bit of an idea…"

Anne was still crying with joy. "Thank you so much. All of you."

"We're glad to be travelling with you, Anne girl. Now we best be running to catch up to our wagons," Mrs. Morgan called out.

"Honestly, Logan, they are the sweetest women I know."

"Well, I know one sweeter," Logan said. He grinned.

Anne blushed. *That man. He seems to love saying things that make me blush.*

They had been traveling for days in the Salt River Range Valley. The mountain peaks around them towered into the sky. The scenery was spectacular.

That night, once they had the dinner boiling in a pot over the fire, they were surprised to see a group of Indians approaching on horseback. It was obvious from the bundles tied to their horses they were fur traders and trappers. The men smiled as they climbed off their painted ponies. They wordlessly sat by the fire, warming their hands. One of the men finally spoke.

"Food." He pointed at the stew bubbling in the cauldron. Mrs. Morgan smiled as she served them huge bowls of stew. The six pioneers and the six Indians sat smiling at each other as they ate their dinner.

The men handed their empty bowls to Mrs. Morgan. She was about to put them in the washing pail when one of the men stopped her. His eyes looked pleading. "Food," he requested. Mrs. Morgan filled their bowls again. The little hunting party appeared to be starving.

"Sleep," one of the men announced. They pulled their blankets off their ponies and two crawled under each wagon. "Thank You, Lord, for more men to protect us," Mrs. Morgan said.

The next morning was a repeat of the night before. The men sat by the fire and watched Mrs. Wilson cook breakfast. They smiled as she handed them plates filled with biscuits, bacon, and eggs. After breakfast, the men walked to their ponies, then walked back with the most beautiful beaded moccasins Anne had ever seen. Each man held a pair…then handed them out to a traveler. The gift was so extravagant—worth so much more than two meals. Anne cried.

"Logan, I can't take this. It's too beautiful a gift."

"Please accept it, Anne, or they will be insulted."

Anne smiled as graciously as she could and accepted the gift. The Indian brave beamed. Once the gifts had been given the men turned to leave. Anne called out, "Wait!" They probably had no idea what wait meant, but they waited patiently anyway. Anne ran to her pantry and produced a sack of apples for the men. She no longer craved them. The men accepted the gift and smiled as they rode off the same way they came.

The travelers all agreed that was an interesting meeting.

As they approached the Salt River Anne was tempted to be fearful. Crossing rivers was extremely dangerous. Oxen often panic in deep, swift water so they try to escape the yoke. This is a treacherous time and can cause wagons to overturn.

The settlers gathered to pray before they were to cross the river.

"Lord," Logan prayed. "You see this river looks mighty swift. We're trusting You to keep us safe."

CHAPTER ELEVEN

Little Sandy Creek, Wyoming
May 1882

The strangest thing happened. When they opened their eyes after they finished praying, they saw the Indians they had fed sitting in canoes in the river waiting for them. They held a raft secured with strong ropes. The Indians pulled the wagons across one by one on the raft. It was incredible. They would not have survived the river crossing if it wasn't for these kind men. Mr. Wilson, Mr. Morgan, and Logan hugged the Indians.

The women hunted in their wagons for gifts to give the men. They found a wind-up clock, a pistol with some shells, some extra-large cauldrons, a sack of cornmeal, and a large hunting knife. Anne really had nothing to give.

"Logan, can you help me break into William's trunk so I can find gifts for a man?"

"Of course."

One man did not get a gift. He looked surprised. It was

hilarious—watching the women pantomiming drinking tea and waiting for a gift to try to explain the situation to the Indians. They laughed when they understood and sat down for some of Mrs. Wilson's notoriously strong and sweet tea. They drank it gratefully while probably wondering why gunshots came from one of the wagons.

Anne finally had a reason to look in William's trunk. He kept it locked and the key was always around his neck. Now that she thought more about it, that was pretty strange. She asked Logan to open the trunk. It took a couple shots to get the lock off.

When they cracked the lid open, Anne was shocked to see a stack of wanted posters lying on the top. They clearly said William Ryan was wanted for bank robbery and murder.

The posters had the names of various forts and settlements along the Oregon Trail. William must have taken them down when they arrived at each settlement. So, that's why he always had a mask over his face. Anne thought it was because of the dust.

She was shocked to see several large bars of gold under the posters. "You were right, Logan. He was a thief. How do we return the gold to the people this was stolen from?"

"Well, that might be very difficult now. We don't rightly know who it belongs to. I guess it's yours."

"But I don't want it."

"Well, we can talk to a judge at the next fort—if there's one there."

Anne pulled out the pile of posters and looked further into the trunk. There were several more gold bars. Anne grieved at the thought that many were without their pay—maybe families had gone hungry—in order for those gold bars to be in this trunk.

Under the gold were piles of very fancy men's clothing.

"Logan, please help me with this clothing."

They walked out to the Indians with arms full of very expensive silk shirts. The men just stared. Anne started handing them clothing. "Here, it's for you. Thank you for your kindness."

The men laughingly carried off armloads of shirts.

The Sweetwater River had to be crossed several more times before reaching the South Pass. Anne left off counting how many times they had to cross. Thankfully there weren't any more treacherous spots. They all rejoiced at God's kindness in sending the Indians to help them in the most dangerous place. Maybe they were angels?

The usual plan was to go to bed at dusk and get up around 4:00 am. That night, it was barely dusk and the weary travelers were fast asleep. If they hadn't been so exhausted, they would have heard two men riding into the camp.

Logan awoke to the sound of shouting and rifle shots.

He crept out from under the wagon and whispered in the wagon doorway, "Anne, you'd best stay in the wagon. I don't know what's happening, but I surely don't want you in the middle of it."

Thankfully it was dark. Logan climbed behind a huge boulder not far from the wagon. Mr. Wilson snuck behind a boulder on the other side of his wagon.

Two masked men sat on their horses in the middle of the camp. They held blazing torches high in the air. "Bring out your money and your women!" one of the men shouted. He sounded like he was drunk—his words were slurred and barely recognizable.

"Don't move or we'll shoot," Mr. Wilson hollered.

Anne peeked from behind the curtain.

One of the bandits ignored Mr. Wilson and grinned into the air as he hollered, "Got any gold or women?" He seemed to be slipping sideways in his saddle. The men were definitely drunk.

A voice came from behind a boulder on the side of the trail. "This is a US Marshal. There's members of the 3rd US Infantry Army battalion right behind you."

That's the truth. Mr. Wilson and Mr. Morgan are soldiers on their way to a new posting.

"I suggest you drop your weapons now or you're both dead men," Logan hollered.

"How do we know you ain't lyin'?" one of the thieves called out.

A voice from behind the men said, "You'd best do it now or we'll shoot you both."

Mr. Morgan and Mr. Wilson pointed their guns at the men. They shot over their heads to let them know they were there and were serious. The horses reared. One of the men fell off.

He made a move towards Anne's wagon. Maybe he hoped to find someone to use as a hostage? Logan didn't think twice. That was the last move that would-be thief ever made. The other bandit immediately dropped his weapon. What happened next was a freak accident. When the gun hit the ground, the muzzle discharged its shot into the bandit's chest. He died on the spot.

Logan ran to Anne. "Are you alright?"

"I'm fine, Logan. Just shocked to see these men who were trying to steal from us lying dead."

"It doesn't pay to live a life of crime—now or in the next life. Now excuse me, ma'am, I have two criminals to bury before the wolves smell their blood."

Even though it was the middle of the night, Anne was too agitated to sleep. She lit a lantern and placed it on a shelf near the trunk. William's wanted posters had obviously been hidden there under lock and key so she wouldn't see them. It was the first time she really allowed herself to believe that her husband was a thief and a murderer—maybe more. She shuddered to think what life would have been like with him.

She looked at the posters more closely. Her husband was also known as "Whiskey Head" Bill Ryan. She knew he drank whiskey—but to have that as a nickname? He had another alias, Tom Hall. Who was this man?

Another poster called him that damned Irishman. *I didn't know he was Irish.* One poster said a gang member had been captured, and named the people in Jesse James' gang to the posse in exchange for his freedom. He told the posse William Ryan shot and killed a man at Muscle Shoals during a robbery.

How long would it have been before his dark side showed up? She had a glimpse of it just before he died. That side was ugly—

nasty—cold. She had never seen that side of him before. Was he playing with her all this time—pretending to be a man of integrity— someone he really was not? Perhaps she would have made an innocent remark that would have triggered his anger and the real William Ryan would have made an appearance?

Anne shuddered again. Now she knew the truth. She didn't need any more proof. How different everything looked. Logan wasn't the horrible monster she thought he was. It was her husband who was actually the beast.

Lord, I see now what happened with William. Logan was defending himself and his deputy. I totally forgive him. Actually, there's nothing to forgive. He did nothing wrong. William was exactly who Logan said he was—a thief and a murderer. Forgive me Lord for hating him—for wanting revenge.

When Logan came back to the wagon, she wanted to rush into his arms and ask for forgiveness. "Logan, I looked at the posters."

"And what did you find?"

"William was clearly the man you said he was."

"What did it say?"

"He had several aliases. He was wanted for bank robbery and horse theft. One of the gang was captured and told the posse William murdered the man at Muscle Shoals."

Anne suddenly felt faint. Logan reached out to steady her. He didn't dare put his arm around her. Not here. Not now. Not in the middle of the night.

"I am so sorry, Logan. I understand now why you shot William. I'm sorry I was so mad at you for so long. I see it all clearly now. Please forgive me for ever being bitter against you."

"Anne, I've already forgiven you. There's nothing left to forgive. It must have been a horrible shock to see your husband lying dead."

"It was a terrible shock."

Lord, I'm so thankful for Logan. He is such a good man.

"It's been an eventful day. Try to get some sleep, Anne."

"Night Logan."

Lord, I don't even begin to know what to say. You saved me from something that could have been Hell on Earth. I'm sorry I didn't know if I could trust You. Thank You.

It was decided the next day would be a day of rest. It was a lovely spring day—a perfect day to bathe in the river. Anne left her outer petticoat on a low branch of a big old oak. She left her undergarments on and tiptoed over the rocks to the river.

Dipping her toes into the frigid water, Anne thought maybe heating water in a cauldron over the fire and bathing in a tin tub wasn't such a bad idea after all.

Anne scrubbed with old brown soap. *Why does it have to smell so terrible?* It pretty much took your skin off, but at least a body felt clean.

Thankfully, she still had a clean dress to put on. She finally had a day to wash the dress she had been wearing since Fort Laramie. Scrubbing the dirty dress on rocks seemed to easily get all the dirt out, but left huge holes in the fabric.

It was so nice to have a toothbrush, even if it was made from bone and boar bristles. She was thankful she hadn't lost any teeth as so many of her friends had.

Some folk chewed on twigs or mint leaves to clean their teeth. Once Logan found some leaves he thought were mint and chewed them into a wad before he discovered they were actually stinging nettles.

"Logan, I made some toothpaste for us. Would you like to try it?"

"Is it safe?"

Anne laughed. "I'm not sure. I figured maybe you could try it first and let me know."

"Very funny. What did you make it from?"

"I just used what was handy—soap, salt, mint leaves, and chalk."

"You're sure it's mint leaves?"

"Positive."

"It sounds kind of disgusting—but for you, I'll try it."

Logan spit out the toothpaste and made sounds like he was dying.

Anne laughed. "Your teeth look so white and clean."

The men decided to go hunting. Buffalo ran in herds of thousands, but six people didn't need such a huge animal. The men trudged over lush grass where masses of gooseberry bushes grew thick along the creeks. Logan shot a couple of sage hens. The men were surprised they were the size of large turkeys. Deer were plentiful so they arrived back with a fine buck. There was feasting that night. The leftover deer and hens were cut into thin strips and dried over the fire as jerky.

The following day there was a downpour. The oxen and wagons slid over the ground as it turned into slimy mud. The wagon wheels were so coated with mud they wouldn't turn any further. They had another day of rest. The weary travelers had no idea how badly they would need that day.

CHAPTER TWELVE

Dear Diary,

The view from the mountains into the Red Bear Valley is breathtaking. Thank You, God, for creating such beauty. The valley is covered with massive trees and thick grass. To say the Bear River is swift and deadly seems an understatement. We followed it most of the day. I can't see how a body could survive if they fell into those waters. When we got to the fork of the Thomas River, we had to ferry across for one dollar. There's no way a wagon would survive in those treacherous waters.

Logan kindly let me ride his horse, so I'm getting the hang of riding. Thankfully, I'm not in a town so I don't have to ride sideways in the saddle like a proper lady. How a woman can hang on sitting like that is beyond me.

People waved at us as we passed a Shoshone village. I have never seen such dark-skinned people. The little ones hid behind their mothers and peeked at us from behind their deerskin skirts with their huge dark eyes. I can see why they call us the white man.

Rena Groot

Logan found a good spot to camp. I could have camped there for life because it was so beautiful—even though the mosquitoes were ferocious. Logan said this would be a good place for our exhausted cattle to feed and rest before our steep climb up the Rocky Mountains. The men went off to fish while the women washed clothes. The men brought back a basket of sleek trout. They said the river was full of fish. Lord, thank You for Your abundant provision.

After dinner a family of Bannock Indians came to say hello. They were even darker skinned than the Indians I had seen earlier. They spoke a few words of English, which was very helpful. They rode on fine Paint ponies, leading a couple of ponies behind them. The man who seemed to be the leader asked if we wanted to buy the ponies. We had no need of them so we thanked them and gave them tea. I am getting good at pantomiming. It was an interesting visit.

The sunset was so beautiful I almost cried. Lord, You are so creative. The beauty of Your handiwork leaves me in awe of You. How can anyone say there is no God?

A massive grizzly lumbered past our camp last night. He stood up on his hind feet to get a good look at us, sniffed the air, then fell forward on his massive paws and moved off. We knew he was a grizzly bear because of the huge hump on his back. I'm thankful the smells from our dinner didn't entice him to join us. He must know this place is called Bear River, as he seemed quite at home here.

The deer are thick among the trees. I have never seen so many. This is a rich area, filled with wildlife.

Logan and I sat by the fire long after the others had gone to bed. I feel so safe when he is near. We talked about the beauty of the trail—then somehow the conversation turned to William. I wasn't sure why, but it seemed right to explain things to Logan. Here's how the conversation went.

"William arrived in Missouri about a month before I did. He purchased a wagon and outfitted it for the trek across the continent. I shudder now to think where the money came from to purchase everything."

"It must be hard to realize the money was stolen from others."

"It is hard. The day after we wed, we were on the trail with about forty other wagons. This was the fresh start I'd been praying for. The possibilities for the future brought me so much hope and joy."

"Why did you leave Independence? Missouri is a beautiful state."

"I had to get away if I wanted a life of my own. I'm not complaining—just telling you the facts. For as long as I can remember, I helped care for my fourteen younger siblings. It was a miracle my mother let me go to school. My life at home was one of servitude. My memories of home are of endless cooking and cleaning."

"That must have been a hard life."

"It was very hard—for more reasons than one. I don't know if my mother ever saw me as her daughter. She never once said she loved me. I don't recall her ever hugging me. I wasn't abused physically—just treated as if I only existed to work."

I wondered why I was saying so much to this man? My husband of three months didn't know any of this about me. What is it about this man that makes me feel like I can talk to him about anything and he will listen and understand?"

"Didn't your father do anything to protect you?"

"My father was a quiet man, kind of a shadow floating through life sort of person. I only saw him at meals. It seemed painful for him to talk to us or even look at his family. He escaped immediately after meals to the barn. He seemed happier there."

"What was your family like, Logan?"

"My father was a rancher. He was a good man—loved God and his family. I never heard him say an unkind word to anyone."

"That's pretty amazing."

"Yup. The only time I saw him get mad was when his horse purposely stepped on his foot."

"What happened then?"

"He hauled off and punched the horse in the shoulder. Knocked him off balance. I think the horse was pretty surprised. He was the most obedient horse you ever saw after that. I think that must have been the only time he ever hit anything. My father is the finest man I ever met."

"Goodnight, Logan."

"Goodnight, Anne."

Dear Diary,

With each day that passes, we see soaring mountain peaks, deep gorges, plummeting waterfalls, sparkling lakes and rivers. The landscape is a continual feast for the eyes. I had never even imagined such beauty existed. I am in constant awe of the majesty and creativity of God.

There have been times the trail was difficult to find. We had to guess where it was and hoped we were traveling in the right direction. Other times it was easy to see, as it was marked with gravestones and litter. It's surprising to see all the things people threw away to lighten their loads.

When we stopped for the night beside the Bear River, we were surprised to see two young Shoshone women ride into our camp. The women were beautiful. Their thick, braided black hair went to their waists and was tied back with beaded straps of deer leather. Their jackets, skirts, and moccasins were intricately beaded. There was a string of ponies behind them. One of the women had a papoose, a sweet, chubby-faced little baby, strapped to her back. It was obvious they wanted us to buy the ponies, and seemed very sad when we said no. All of our communication was by pantomime—as we didn't speak Shoshone and they didn't speak English.

We realized the advancing throngs of white settlers would disrupt their ancestral way of life. It grieved our hearts to realize we were part of the problem. We gave the women gifts—bags of rice and cornmeal—for which they seemed very grateful. As they rode away with their string of ponies, it made me wonder about their lives—so different from mine. I didn't think I would survive if I had to live their lives.

Some days the cold breath of the snowy mountaintops blew

down on us. Was that a warning that an early winter could be expected? We hope to be in Oregon long before the snow flurries begin. I am so enjoying the mountain air—so fresh and clean. The river baths in the cold water are invigorating.

Somehow, even though the trail is rough and the days long, I am thankful to God I made this journey. It is giving me a taste of health and peace I didn't know existed—and freedom. For the first time in my life, I feel free. Free to be who I am. Somehow, in these mountains, with all the fresh air—the sunshine—the trees—the flowing rivers—the majestic mountains—all past pains and sorrows have dissolved. I can breathe. I feel the presence of God.

Later that morning, while bumping along in the wagon, Anne decided to write more of her thoughts and impressions of the trip.

We were surprised to see a community of homesteads in what seemed to be the middle of nowhere. Wagons loaded with lumber were coming down from the heights of the Uintah Mountains. We were also surprised to see a railroad being built from Evanston to Bear River. It made us sad, knowing this pristine beauty was about to be replaced with houses, factories, lumber yards, and trains. The wild beauty was being marred.

There was a mercantile in the midst of the homesteads, so we stopped to see what was available. The women of the area knitted hats, scarves, and mittens. We all decided to buy some just in case the weather decided to surprise us. They told us the Rocky Mountains had a mind of its own, and even in summer there could be raging, unexpected snowstorms. We picked up some supplies to replenish our food. As we were about to leave the little settlement, one of the men of the town offered to guide us through the mountain pass. He said it could be treacherous. We were thankful for his kind offer.

Once we were far from the settlement, out of danger of anyone hearing him, he told us some things to be aware of. He warned us that the dried eggs we purchased had probably never seen a chicken and the dried milk had never seen a cow. What on earth was it that we bought, then? It's crazy what some people will do to make a dollar. How thankful we were that man took it upon himself to "guide" us. We buried the "egg" and "milk" powder so no wild animals would find the stash of whatever it was and die.

There was one time in our travels along the Bear River we heard a woman screaming. The men hurried off to help the damsel in distress. My thoughts were, why was a woman off in the wilderness, and of course, why was she screaming? Thankfully, they took their rifles along. Who knew mountain lions have the same cry as a woman? The cat apparently stalked the men and leaped out of a tree on Mr. Wilson. Logan shot it before it could hurt him. I'm so glad I didn't go along on that rescue mission.

The mountain sheep clinging to the sides of the rocks are fascinating. Sometimes, it looks like they are standing on air. How they find the tiny crevices to step on is incredible. I have seen the beauty of God's creation like I could never have imagined it back in Independence. It seems like I lived such a dreary, boring life there. This is so exciting—to see the vast, mostly unknown spaces of God's creation. Thank You, Lord, for bringing me here.

We stopped for the night under a huge cleft on the side of the mountain. It was a good thing we did, as it poured that night. The rock ledge was so big, our wagons were mostly safe and dry. The next morning was Sunday. The sun arose warm and bright, so we decided to rest and enjoy the beauty of the day. Mrs. Wilson made a fabulous breakfast of quail's eggs, deer jerky, and biscuits.

The coffee was delicious with fresh cream from our cow and wild honey. Thankfully, our cow still gives us milk, even though she's probably exhausted from all her travels. Should an exhausted cow still give milk? I have no idea. We keep telling her how much we appreciate her and her milk, so maybe that encourages her. Who knows? Do animals understand us? Will they understand us in heaven?

This land is so beautiful, Lord. Your creation is breathtaking. Last night, after the fire died down, I decided to walk around the camp in the moonlight. The mosquitoes hummed their songs in my ears and the night birds called to their mates. A few bats flew overhead—hopefully planning to gorge on mosquitoes. *Logan must have heard me*—as he got up and we sat on logs by the dying embers—completely in awe of the spectacular beauty around us.

My heart is full. I am at peace—knowing God is with me. I hear God speaking to my spirit. He is saying, "My presence will go with you, and I will give you rest."[13]

I have heard that many died on this trail—many turned back because the journey was too hard—but I feel Your strength, Your presence—all around me and in me, Lord. I know You will go before me and will be with me; You will never leave or forsake me. I will not be afraid. I will not be discouraged.[14]

I know You are here. I hear Your voice in the wind. I feel Your presence in the beauty that surrounds me. I choose to trust you and not be afraid. I don't know what the future holds. Will I be alone and impoverished? Will I ever find a home? I don't know—but I know no matter what—You will be with me. You once told Joshua, a mighty general, a leader of Your people, "Have not I commanded You? Be strong and courageous. Do not be afraid: do not be discouraged, for the Lord your God will be with you wherever you go." I believe that is Your Word for me too—and I trust You, Mighty God.

---

[13] Exodus 33:14
[14] Deuteronomy 31:8

CHAPTER THIRTEEN

Soda Springs, Rocky Mountains, Idaho
June 1882

Dear Diary,

The pine-clad mountains surrounded us as we traveled East. The fragrance of evergreens filled the air as we followed a gravelly stream bed for a day. It was strange how at times the air smelled like rotten eggs. Mr. Wilson said it smelled like sulphur. He seemed excited—said he had heard about the horrible smells—and was delighted it was a sign we were getting close to the hot pools. He said we would have hot baths and hot water to wash clothes. It sounded too good to be true. If only it didn't smell so terrible.

We came upon a deep pool with the clearest deep, blue-green water you could imagine. Mr. Wilson said the sun reflecting off the sulphur and minerals made the beautiful hue. The whole scene was breathtakingly gorgeous. We decided to camp by the hot pools for a day. Sadly, by the time we camped, the darkness closed in so we couldn't bathe.

The smells from the crackling fire masked the smell of sulphur.

The long, drawn-out howl of a wolf made a mournful sound that made me shudder. His friends replied—their lonely howls came from the trees surrounding us.

Logan didn't help when he started howling with them. He may have thought it funny—but what if he actually invited them to join us for dinner? Mrs. Wilson informed him she wasn't amused. It wasn't until we saw the shining eyes in the bushes around us that Logan gave up his wolf serenade. Logan decided maybe sleeping under the wagon that night wasn't the wisest idea—so he slept on the wagon seat. I'm sure it must have been uncomfortable, but much preferred to being eaten alive.

Bathing in the lovely hot water the next morning was so delightful. Had a bath ever felt so good? My hair felt like silk after washing it in the mineral rich water. I usually wore it in a braid down my back, but it felt so good just to let it flow.

Logan watched me a lot all day. If Logan was the marrying kind, any girl would be honored to be his wife. Is he lonely, Lord? It must create an ache in his heart knowing he will never marry.

While sitting in the pool, we saw herds of mountain goats scaling the cliffs above us. If any lost their footing, I wonder if they would have fallen on our heads.

I noticed my skirts and petticoats were wearing thin—obviously washing clothes on rocks is hard on fabric. Thankfully, Mrs. Morgan noticed my shabby wardrobe and invited me to her wagon. She was bigger than me, and had a few extra frocks to share. Getting new dresses was a blessing. She said she didn't want anything for her dresses—but it was fun secretly leaving bags of potatoes and rice on her wagon seat. I definitely got the better end of that bargain. Being a seamstress, Mrs. Morgan's clothes were sewn with such care. She made the tiniest stitches I've ever seen. Thank You, God, for my beautiful new frocks.

My kid boots also wore thin from all the walking. Why hadn't I thought to bring an extra pair? Large holes gaped at me from the soles—too big to be patched or stuffed with cloth any longer. I wanted to keep my beautiful beaded Indian moccasins for a special occasion, but saving my feet seemed pretty special. The deer skin felt so soft and comfortable I never wanted to take them off. The soles had several layers of surprisingly tough hide. I had never seen such beautiful moccasins.

Thank You, God, for how You care for people. I needed dresses and shoes and You provided them. It reminds me of the verse, "And why take ye thought for raiment? Consider the lilies of the field, how they grow; they toil not, neither do they spin: And yet I say unto you, that even Solomon in all his glory was not arrayed like one of these."[15]

Mr. Wilson suggested that seeing we were having a resting day, we should go for a hike up the mountains to see the view. I'm not sure how he came up with such an idea. Did he forget about the wolves? Maybe he thought the hours of walking every day on the trail wasn't enough?

I didn't want to be left alone at the camp—so, the six of us set off in the early afternoon, following an animal trail. We planned to walk until we got to a place to view the valley. The hike was pleasant—until we met the wolf pack. Don't wolves usually sleep during the day and come out to hunt at night? Someone forgot to tell them.

These were massive timber wolves—watching us from either side of the trail. Their coats camouflaged them—blending well with the colors of the trees. Logan called out, "Whatever you do—don't be afraid. Wolves can smell fear." Right. Was he kidding? My heart was already pounding in my chest. I kept saying a Bible verse over and over—"When I am afraid, I will trust in You".[16]

Logan called out that now might be a good time to return to camp. Mr. Wilson thought perhaps we should climb a bit higher—the clearing must be close —but five voices disagreed with him.

The men walked at the front, the middle, and the back of our little group. Thankfully, they brought rifles. Did the wolves sense the

---

[15] Matthew 6:28-29
[16] Psalm 56:3

men were armed? *I didn't make eye contact with any of the animals, I thought that might be considered a challenge, so I tried to look straight ahead as I walked. The campsite never looked so welcome.*

Mr. Morgan said for future adventures we should stick to the trail. All agreed—except Mr. Wilson—who thought the walk had been lovely. I told him mountain climbing was better suited to mountain goats—not to women in moccasins and petticoats.

As Mrs. Morgan and I prepared the evening supper, wolf eyes watched us from the shadows.

As the days passed, the further we travelled, the colder the air became. That wasn't surprising as we were high in the mountains. We draped ourselves in buffalo hides to keep warm. From a distance, when it got darker and it was harder to discern shapes clearly, I think we must have looked like a bunch of bears huddled around the fire. They are actually called a sleuth of bears—but I prefer bunch of bears.

The wagons seemed to groan more these days—maybe because the axle grease was so cold? The oxen were more obstinate, not as willing to pull the heavy loads. Grass for them was a bit harder to find. Some days I walked ahead of them with carrots strung across my back—to keep the oxen plodding towards the elusive food. At the end of the day, they were rewarded with the carrots.

One of the horses that had been tethered to the back of Mr. Wilson's wagon, suddenly seemed fed up with the monotony of the trail. He reared up, broke the rope away from the wagon, and disappeared into the bush. He must have ripped his jaw in his attempt to escape, as there was blood on the back of the wagon. There was no point of chasing him. He could have gone anywhere. Perhaps the wolves smelled his blood and dined on horse meat that night.

At one point we reached a clearing where we could see the trail winding up higher into the mountains. A deep gorge appeared to the right of the trail. Logan flashed me one of his reassuring smiles, as if to say, "It's okay. We'll be fine. God's protecting us." As we passed the gorge, Logan called out, "Don't look down, Anne." Thankfully the oxen are sure-footed and we made it past that terrifying spot.

Lord, I'm worried—again—about what will become of me. I'm sorry I'm not trusting You more. I know You are faithful. I know You can provide for me. But, sometimes I feel scared, Lord. I feel so alone. Thank You, Logan is here—but that's right now. What about when we arrive in Oregon City and he leaves? Please help me trust You.

They passed a wagon train heading East. *Why on earth would people want to go east?* Logan talked with some of the folks briefly. One of the men told him they were Mormon missionaries. They felt the need to go back to Salt Lake City area—felt it was a better place for them to raise their children. They were disappointed with what they found in Oregon—too much worldliness—saloons and brick houses. It wasn't the peaceful, innocent communities they hoped to find.

One of the men said, "There's a treacherous river crossing ahead. A family of ours attempted to cross the river on a ferry. The oxen panicked—lunged forward—pulled the wagon into the river—the ferry capsized. The entire family of seven are lost."

"My condolences to you, sir," Logan said.

"Thank you, son." The man wiped the dust off his pants before he carried the water barrel back to his wagon. The wagon trains waved goodbye to each other as we headed off in opposite directions.

"Well, I guess the grass does seem greener on the other side," Mrs. Wilson said as she helped peel potatoes for supper. "We think we're headed to a better place...but are we?"

Mrs. Morgan asked, "I wonder what we'll find in Oregon?" Anne must have been quiet for too long—so the women looked at her as if waiting for a reply.

"Well, I don't know what to expect. I really have nowhere to go. I know no one. Today, I'm wondering why I'm even here."

Mrs. Morgan said, "God knows why you're here, Anne girl. He's leading you. He will show you the way."

That night, Anne couldn't sleep. The wolves howling kept her awake.

Why do they have to sound so mournful? Why did that missionary have to tell us about the shallow grave on the trail dug up by wolves?

What's to become of me? I have no money—the gold in William's trunk doesn't belong to me. I have nowhere to go...no home...no one. God, even if William was a scoundrel—life would have been easier with a man to protect me. Why did he have to die? I know—I saw the posters. He was an evil man. But, God—I have no one but You in this world. Would you please protect me? Please hold me close to Your heart, Lord. I'm sorry...but I'm so scared.

Anne gave up trying to sleep and lit a lantern. Even though it was the middle of the night, she picked up her Bible and asked God to lead her to an encouraging word. She opened the pages to this verse, *"Wherein ye greatly rejoice, though now for a season, if need be, ye are in heaviness through manifold temptations: that the trial of your faith, being much more precious than of gold that perisheth, though it be tried with fire, might be found unto praise and honour and glory at the appearing of Jesus Christ: whom having not seen, ye love; in whom, though now ye see him not, yet believing, ye rejoice with joy unspeakable and full of glory: receiving the end of your faith, even the salvation of your souls."*

Lord, what are my "manifold temptations"? Does that mean I am tempted to mistrust You? If so, that's true. That's pretty much a daily battle. Do I trust You? It's hard when I look at what the future might hold for me. How will I live? Will I have to get a job as a washerwoman and live in poverty all the days of my life? I am trying to trust Your plans for me are good—but in all honesty—I don't know if I believe that.

A voice at the wagon door startled her. "Anne, are you okay?"

"I'm fine, Logan. I couldn't sleep."

"Why?"

"I'm worried about the future. I don't know what God has in store for me. I have nowhere to go, Logan. I'm wondering if this whole thing has been one huge mistake. Maybe I should have stayed in Independence…"

"Anne, I believe God has good things in store for you. He loves you, Anne girl. He will look after you. Trust Him."

"That's easy for you to say. You have a job as a marshal—a place to go—people who need you. I have nothing."

"Trust God. He loves you. He will take care of you."

"It's hard."

"May I pray for you, Anne?"

"Please."

"Dear God, please comfort Anne's heart. Help her know she can trust You. Thank You, Lord."

"Thank you."

"You're welcome. Try to get some sleep. We are headed for Fort Boise tomorrow. It'll be a long day."

"Night, Logan."

"Night, Anne."

Anne blew out the lantern and crawled under the cozy feather quilt Logan made for her. She fell asleep talking to God. *Lord, how does he do it? That man calms my heart like no one ever has. Thank You for bringing Logan into my life.*

CHAPTER FOURTEEN

Among the prairie dogs in Idaho
June 1882

"Anne, would you like to go fishing?" Logan asked.

"I'd love to."

The walk to the river was fascinating. There was so much to see. Prairie flowers of every hue dotted the path. Anne had no idea jackrabbits could be so huge. Deer with wide-eyed fawns peered at them from behind gooseberry bushes. Hawks and osprey circled overhead, looking for gophers to pounce on. Prairie dogs–and their holes—were everywhere. Obviously, no predators would starve in these parts.

Anne was so busy looking at everything she didn't notice the hole in the ground. Thankfully, before she had a chance to do any damage, Logan grabbed her arm and swung her away from danger

Dear Diary,

This is kind of a funny story—although I'm sure the poor gopher wasn't amused. Logan cast his fishing line behind him so he could cast it far out into deep water. He was surprised when the line didn't cast forward as it was supposed to. Obviously, it snagged on something behind him. When he turned around to look, he was dismayed to see he had snagged a young gopher. The critter wouldn't let Logan near to free it from the fish hook, so he apologized to the prairie dog, cut the line, and wished him the best of luck.

The landscape in Idaho is harsh—the Bear River and Snake River crossings treacherous. The river has many whirlpools and deep holes where a wagon could easily get stuck or overturned. Is this where so many lost their lives, Lord?

The descent into some of the valleys is so steep wagon wheels have to be tied together. This locks the wheels so the wagons don't roll forward into the back of the oxen as they descend the trail. The Wilsons found out the hard way about their need to lock the wheels. Two of their oxen were badly maimed by the wagon hurling forward and ramming into the back of their legs. The poor animals had to be shot. The only good thing about that is we had a day of rest—if you can call it that because we worked from before dawn until after dusk—making jerky out of the oxen.

The Oregon Trail and the California Trail divided again. One trail headed South and one North. There seemed to be a few places where that happened along the trail. Did some pioneer decide, "Oh, I think I'll go South now?" So many carved their own trails it was difficult to know which was the right way to go. Tracks went in all directions.

"Anne, this is your final chance to decide. Oregon or California?"

"You know full well I can't drive a team of oxen by myself. You know I need a strong man to help me. You said you're going to Oregon, so I'm going there too. I would die without you."

I think he just wanted to hear me say I couldn't live without him. I was so surprised at what he said next. "Anne, if you want to go to California, I wouldn't leave you. I'd go with you and protect you." Of course, my heart melted when he said that. I hope he knows I meant it when I said, "Logan, you are such a good friend. Thank you for your kindness."

Strangely, we ran out of tracks to follow—so we were lost for a few days. They just disappeared. We ended up in a place with a sign that said, "City of Rocks". It was incredibly beautiful—unlike anything I had ever seen. Magnificent rock formations spiraled up to Heaven. The granite and limestone formations were spectacular. We mushed the oxen through the area—staring in wide-eyed wonder as we traveled. It was like we had stepped into another world.

It was funny how we finally found the trail. We just had to look for litter. Some unscrupulous merchants sold settlers way more supplies than they could possibly ever use, so parts of the trail became a junk heap. Because wagons had to be as light as possible to ferry across the Snake River, many discarded barrels of food— mostly bacon for some crazy reason. Wagon parts littered the land—mostly spare wheels and metal rims. Broken down wagons and oxen's bones, abandoned furniture and books littered the trail. When we couldn't see tracks, we simply followed the junk.

This is strange—so I want to include it in my diary. In 1862, President Lincoln announced the Emancipation Proclamation, which would become law in January, 1863. Slaves were given freedom. So, here it was 1882, nearly twenty years later, and a man mushed a group of about seven black-skinned folk through the rocks.

The people looked at us with huge, sorrowful eyes as they trudged past. This was wrong. I asked Logan to do something— anything—arrest somebody—shoot them if necessary. I didn't understand why a US marshal couldn't arrest the man for breaking the terms of the Proclamation, and why he couldn't set those slaves free. He said this wasn't his jurisdiction and he had no authority there to arrest anyone. It was hard to admit the situation was hopeless. If I was trudging along in chains, I'd want someone to come to my rescue. I think Logan realized I was disappointed he didn't do something for those people. We didn't talk for the rest of the day.

As we sat at the campfire that night, Logan said, "Anne, there was nothing I could do for those people."

I didn't believe him. "Have you read, Uncle Tom's Cabin?"

"Can't say I have..."

"Well, you need to read it."

"What's it about?"

"Harriet Beecher Stowe met enslaved people trying to escape on something called the Underground Railroad. She wrote a book about it called Uncle Tom's Cabin. Folks say that book sparked the Civil War. I'm surprised you haven't heard of it."

"What's the Underground Railroad?"

"A group of people—white and black—color didn't matter—used their time, talents, and treasure to help folks escape slavery."

"Where was it?"

"It went from the deep South, all the way into Canada"

"I'm sorry, Anne. I would love to have helped those folks, but there was nothing I could do."

Lord, I'm disappointed with Logan. I thought he was a knight in shining armor. It's sad to realize he can't right all wrongs we come across—he's just a man. Please help me see him—and all people—through Your eyes.

It rained all night. The next day, the smell of lavender and wild roses sweetened the air. The trail was muddy—but at least it wasn't thick gumbo.

"So, Anne girl. Are you still mad at me?"

Logan flashed Anne such an innocent smile it was impossible for her to stay mad.

"No, of course not. I realize there was nothing you could do for those poor people besides murder their master."

"Phew! I don't know if I could stand another day without speaking to my dear friend Anne."

My dear friend Anne?

"So, what are your plans for today, Anne?"

What a funny question. The plans are the same as all other days...trudge along beside the wagon. Hmmm...let me see...

"Well, first off, I'm going to give the maids the day off so they can enjoy the day. It's such a glorious day, don't you think?"

"Yes, it's lovely. The maids?"

"Yes. I believe the butler should be given the day off as well. He's been working very hard, helping prepare for my high tea with the Queen."

"You don't say?"

"Yes. I am expecting the queen for high tea around five pm. I do hope she's not late, as the crumpets will be soggy if left buttered too long."

"Well, it sounds like you have some great plans for the day."

"Yes, I expect Queen Victoria will arrive with quite an entourage, so I've asked the bakers to make lots of treats."

"So, they don't get the day off I assume?"

"Oh, heavens no. Someone has to prepare all the pastries."

"Have you any other plans for your day?"

"Yes. I plan to spend an hour pruning the rose bushes before the queen arrives. They are beautiful—but they are getting rather wild looking."

"I see."

"Yes, they need a good cutting back or soon no one will be able to see out the parlor window."

"Right. That makes sense."

"The gardener has also been given the day off, so I'll have to cut back the roses myself. I have cut crystal vases to put the flowers in, so they will look beautiful on the piano."

"The piano?"

"Yes, the one in the parlor."

"Right, that piano."

"What are your plans for today, Logan?"

Logan tapped the back of one of the oxen with the goad. "Our poor oxen are getting tired. Can't say I blame them."

"Your plans for the day…?"

"Right, my plans…let me see."

"I'll be joining you and the queen for high tea in the parlor."

"Oh, no. You can't."

"Why's that?"

"You weren't sent a formal invitation from her royal highness."

"I see. May I help the butler serve tea to you and your guest?

"I suppose, as long as you promise to be very quiet and not disturb the tea party."

"I wouldn't dream of speaking unless spoken to."

"Do you have any other plans, Logan?"

"Yes, I am going to have a polo match with the Prince, right after high tea."

"Really?"

"Yes. He's been asking me for months—so I finally have a spare moment to oblige him."

"That's very good of you. You mustn't beat him too badly. That would be rude."

"It's the least I can do for my country. We need to maintain friendly relations with the royal family, right?"

Anne laughed. "Oh, Logan, you're the best! Thanks for joining me in my little pretend game."

That night, as they sat under trillions of stars, Logan smiled at Anne and asked, "So, how was high tea with the queen?"

The Wilsons and Morgans stared at each other. They heard stories about insanity on the trail.

Logan and Anne burst out laughing. "It was a funny make-believe game we played to help pass the time." Anne said.

"Well, next time you have high tea with the queen, please be sure to invite us."

"Of course. I will." Anne said. Logan winked at her and they burst out laughing again.

Lord, it feels so right to be with Logan. I feel such a kinship with that man—more than a friendship. It's too bad he says he will never marry. Also, I need to remember to hide my diary now. Logan mustn't read it any more.

CHAPTER FIFTEEN

Fort Hall, Idaho
June 1882

They followed the Snake River until they arrived at Fort Hall in Western Idaho. It was much bigger than Anne expected. Naturally, it was a fur trading post.

An old timer sat on a rocking chair in front of the mercantile. He chewed on the end of his corn cob pipe, surveying the strangers.

"Howdy folks. What brings you to Fort Hall?"

Logan answered, "Just travelling through to Oregon City, sir. We were hoping to buy some fresh vegetables."

"Well, you've come to the right place, son. We have some carrots, potatoes, and turnips in the root cellar."

"That sounds mighty fine," Logan answered.

"If the ladies would like to wash up and sleep in a bed tonight, there's a room in the fort with a couple beds—and a room with a single bed."

"I'll let them know. Thank you."

"My wife makes the best rabbit stew you ever tasted. It's fifteen cents for a bowl."

"We'd be happy to have her stew. Thank you," Logan said.

"The name's Nathaniel. Let me know if you need anything."

That night as they sat at supper, Nathaniel told them about the fort.

"This fort was built in 1834 by Nathaniel Wyeth, my grandpa. He was a trapper and fur trader. Sadly, he wasn't able to compete with the powerful Hudson Bay Company, so he sold them the fort in 1837. We stayed on here to run the place."

"What does the fort do now, Nathaniel?" Mr. Morgan asked.

"This here fort is a key stop for the overland stage. The mail and freight lines to the camps and towns are serviced from here. Folks headed to mining camps and frontier stations stop here for supplies." Nathaniel took a deep draw on his pipe.

"It does sound like an important post," Mr. Wilson said.

"It's the most important post in the Snake River Valley—actually, I'd say it's the most important post in the Pacific Northwest."

"I can see why you'd say that," Mr. Wilson said.

Nathaniel grinned at the little party as he scooped up heaping spoons of rabbit stew and piled it into their wooden bowls.

"I'm sure my wife is the best cook this side of the Rockies."

No one argued. Whatever she did to it, the stew was the best rabbit stew they had ever tasted. Her baking powder biscuits fairly melted in your mouth.

"Thank you for your hospitality, Nathaniel," Anne said.

"You're welcome, little lady."

Only one other man ever called her little lady. Thinking of Clayton made her skin crawl.

Nathaniel continued. "It's unfortunate the Hudson Bay Company has such a monopoly on the fur trade. My grandpa couldn't make a go of it—they squeezed him out—undercut his prices for furs to the Indians so they wouldn't trade with him."

"Why didn't your grandfather give the trappers a better deal?" Logan asked.

"He tried. No matter how low he went, the Hudson Bay

Company went lower. Most mountain men ended up working for the big companies. The Hudson Bay Company had a monopoly. If a man tried to make a go of it on their own, they were undercut and went bankrupt. It was nasty."

"That does sound mean," Anne said.

"Also, the British don't want American pioneers in Oregon. The Brits have gone hunting today. They will be back this evening. They tell folks the land is too rough so they should turn back."

"Why, that's insanity," Mr. Morgan said. "We haven't travelled all this way and arrived in Oregon to turn around now."

Mr. Wilson added, "How do they expect to convince us we should turn back?"

"They will show you wagons that have been abandoned from earlier pioneers. They will tell you it's so rough the oxen died—they will show you the bones. They will paint a sad picture of pioneers struggling on by foot without a wagon or animals. They will make it sound very dismal. Don't listen to them and don't tell them I warned you."

"Thanks for the warning," Logan said.

Nathaniel asked, "Gentlemen, would you like to join me in the parlor for cigars and brandy?"

"That would be mighty fine," Mr. Wilson said. Mr. Morgan and Logan said, "Thank you, but we need to tend to our animals."

"There's another gentleman staying at the fort," Nathaniel added. "He said he wouldn't be joining us for dinner. Kind of a strange man. He said something about being from the army in Fort Laramie."

Fort Laramie? It couldn't be…

After dinner, Nathaniel said, "Ladies, my wife will show you to your rooms."

Anne couldn't believe the room. It was beautifully decorated—the fanciest place she had ever seen. A massive wooden four-poster bed nearly filled the room. The coverlet was crocheted with flowers of all different hues. A mahogany washstand had a lovely oval mirror on the wall above it—the frame made from carved roses covered in burnished brass. A fire crackled merrily from a stone fireplace. A massive black bearskin lay on the floor by the fireplace, with a comfortable stuffed chair beside it. There was a brief moment of longing—wishing she had a husband to share all this loveliness with. Anne felt a twinge of sadness realizing that might never be. She buried the thought as she fell onto the bed. She soon fell asleep, wrapped in soft, quilted folds.

Anne was jarred from a deep sleep in the middle of the night. Something felt wrong. What was it?

Lord, am I imagining things?

A noise in the corner of the room made her jump.

"Who's there?"

Something definitely moved in the corner—a dark shadow.

"I said, who's there?"

Something dark walked out of the shadows. The moonlight shining through the window lattice revealed a huge man with an ugly scar across his forehead.

"I said you haven't seen the last of me, little lady."

"Clayton?"

"In the flesh. I deserted Fort Laramie—just to find you."

Anne was horrified. This had to be a terrible dream.

"So, little lady, I have a wagon waiting outside, ready to depart. Get up."

"Why?"

"You're going with me."

"I'm not going anywhere with you."

"Oh, but you must."

"Why?"

"Because, if you don't come with me now, I shall be forced to kill your friend Logan in his sleep."

"You wouldn't dare."

"Would you care to try me and see?"

"No."

"Then let's get going."

"Why are you chasing me?"

"Because I have decided you are the woman for me."

"But, I have decided you are not the man for me."

"We'll see about that. Get up."

"No."

"Get up now. Don't make me mad," Clayton snarled.

Anne got up. She didn't want this lunatic going after Logan.

As they approached the wagon standing ready in the yard, Anne decided this was her last hope to escape. She knew once they were out of the fort, there would be no protection from Clayton. She ran screaming towards the barn.

Dear God, please wake Logan up.

Clayton ran after her.

"Come here, you wretched woman. How dare you defy me?" Clayton hollered.

She was almost at the barn. If only she could reach it...

Strong hands grabbed her by the hair. The pain was excruciating. She screamed again.

Clayton carried her kicking and screaming to the wagon. They were almost there when Anne heard the most wonderful voice she ever heard call out, "Leave her alone, Clayton, or you're a dead man."

Thank You, God, for waking Logan.

Clayton spun Anne around so she was facing Logan. He stood behind her, like the coward he was, with his pistol held to Anne's head.

"Get back in the barn, Logan, and bolt the door shut, or I'll blow her head off."

"So, you're planning to add kidnapping and murder to your attempted rape sentence? Or is murder already on your charges? Did you murder the Indian agent? Was that because he wouldn't go along with your corrupt schemes? Did he refuse to steal from his friends for you?"

"Shut up or I'll blow her head off."

"You can't. You know I'd shoot you now. Or, if you managed to escape, you'd be caught, and you would be hung. Or, you could leave now and I won't chase you."

"Do you think I'm a fool? How do I know I can trust you'd keep your word?"

"I give you my word as an officer in the US Army, a marshal, and most of all—a son of God."

"Very eloquent! Bravo! But in all your talking, you never answered my question."

"And that was?" Logan asked.

"How do I know I can trust you?"

"You don't know and I can't convince you unless you get in the wagon over yonder and get out of here. Then you'll see if I spoke truth or lies."

"Okay, I'll leave." Clayton curled his lip at Anne, "You still haven't seen the last of me, little lady."

"Come near her again, Clayton, and it won't go so well for you. Attempted rape and attempted kidnapping are justifiable offenses for a US marshal to shoot you."

Clayton sneered at Logan, leered at Anne, then snapped the reins over his oxen. When Clayton was finally out of sight, Anne collapsed on the ground.

"Anne!" Logan scooped her up in his arms to carry her back to her room.

"This carrying you around is getting to be a habit…" Then he said under his breath, "But I love it…"

CHAPTER SIXTEEN

Fort Boise on the Snake River, Idaho
June 1882

"Where exactly are we?" Anne asked as they trudged over deep ruts in the trail.

"We should be arriving at Fort Boise in a few hours." Logan replied.

"So, we're still in Idaho?"

"Yes, ma'am."

"How much farther is it to Oregon?"

"That depends entirely on the weather, Anne."

Looking ahead, Anne thought the mountain peaks looked daunting. She thought what a miracle it was trappers ever found their way through those mountains to carve trails. She wondered how many had been trapped by blizzards or lost their way and starved to death. Maybe it was best not to think about those things...

Lord, I won't be afraid. Instead of allowing terrifying thoughts to fill her mind, Anne decided she would think about God's Word.

I will lift up mine eyes unto the hills, from whence cometh my help. My help cometh from the LORD, which made heaven and earth. He will not suffer my foot to be moved: he that keepeth me will not slumber. Behold, he that keepeth Israel shall neither slumber nor sleep. [17] *Lord, please help me trust You.*

They wanted to keep moving after lunch, but there was no way to go forward. They were trapped by the blinding, driving rain. Sitting in the wagon all day was difficult. Anne pulled out a small case of readers she brought along. They were the only thing she had left from her childhood.

"Logan, may I read to you?"

"Well, that sounds like the best offer I've had all morning, next to the hard tack and cold tea that is."

"This story is called *Smiles*."

Logan smiled his beautiful smile. Anne smiled back.

"Poor lame Jennie sat at her window, looking out upon a dismal, narrow street, with a look of pain and weariness on her face."

"That sounds like a sad story," Logan said. "Is there another story that's happier?"

"*Smiles* is a lovely story. It's about a lame girl and a good-hearted boy who brings her flowers, grapes, and smiles."

"It sounds sad, Anne."

"Okay, I'll read *In Time's Swing*. It's a poem about how quickly time passes."

Father Time, your footsteps go
Lightly as the falling snow.
In your swing I'm sitting, see!
Push me softly; one two, three,
Twelve times only. Like a sheet,
Spread the snow beneath my feet,
Singing merrily, let me swing
Out of winter into spring.

Swing me out, and swing me in!

Anne

Trees are bare, but birds begin
Twittering to the peeping leaves,
On the bough beneath the eaves,
Wait,—one lilac bud I saw.
Icy hillsides feel the thaw,
April chased off March today;
Now I catch a glimpse of May.

Oh, the smell of sprouting grass!
In a blur the violets pass,
Whispering from the wildwood come
Mayflowers breath and insects hum.
Roses carpeting the ground;
Thrushes, orioles, warbling sound:—
Swing me low, and swing me high,
To the warm clouds of July.

Lower now, for at my side
White pond lilies open wide.
Underneath the pine's tall spire
Cardinal blossoms burn like fire.
They are gone; the golden-rod
Flashes from the dark green sod,
Crickets in the grass I hear;
Asters light the fading year.

Slower still! October weaves
Rainbows of the forest leaves,
Gentians fringed, like eye of blue,
Glimmer out of sleety dew,
Meadow green I sadly miss;
Winds through weathered sedges hiss,
Oh, 'tis snowing, swing me fast,
While December shivers past!

Frosty-bearded Father Time,
Stop your footfall on the rime!
Hard you push, your hand is rough;
You have swung me long enough.
"Nay, no stopping," say you? Well,
Some of your best stories tell,
While you swing me—gently, do!
From the Old Year to the New.

"Well, what did you think?"
Silence.
"Logan?"
"Logan, are you snoring?"
I can't believe that lovely poem put him to sleep...
That night, the rain finally stopped. It had been pouring for days. The little group sat around the fire—no longer trapped in their wagons. They were thankful the rain had stopped—thankful they could have a hot meal—thankful the blazing fire kept wild animals and the chill of night away. They could hear wolves howling mournfully from the nearby mountain heights, but they were safe by the fire.

Mr. Wilson was the first to speak. "It's hard to imagine this route was blazed by fur traders. How they ever found a way through this wilderness is beyond me." Mr. Wilson reached down and casually picked a tick off his trousers. "There's so many critters in these mountains—ticks to grizzlies—it's a wonder the fur traders made it out alive."

There was silence as Mr. Wilson's words were considered. He spoke up again. "Why are you making this trip, Mr. Morgan?"

Mr. Morgan paused to look at his wife. Her eyes seemed to say, "Go on. Tell them."

"Well, I guess I'm hoping we find a better life. We heard Oregon is a rich land—a land of milk and honey." Mr. Morgan paused to throw another log on the fire. "There was nothing left for us back in Missouri. The depression of 1837 left my family poor.

We continued to farm the land, hoping for a turn around, but the topsoil had been blown away and no matter what we did the land produced poor crops. We hoped for a turn around that never came. So, I joined the army. They posted me to Oregon."

Mr. Wilson spoke up again, "What brings you out West, Logan?"

Logan glanced at Anne and smiled. That smile pretty much said it all. If not for promising to chaperone Anne, he would have stayed at one of the forts. A US marshal was welcome anywhere by decent folks.

"Well, after Anne's husband was killed, I felt duty bound to see her safely to wherever she wanted to go."

Mrs. Morgan and Mrs. Wilson exchanged knowing glances. Their faces said they knew this was more than a man dutifully helping a widow in distress. Every time Logan looked at Anne, their suspicions were confirmed. Mrs. Morgan whispered to Mrs. Wilson, "He forgot to mention the fact he loves the girl and can't bear to let her out of his sight."

Mrs. Wilson spoke up. "That's a mighty fine thing you're doing, Logan. Where's the final destination?"

Logan looked at Anne. "I'm not rightly sure, ma'am, but I'll know when I get there." Everyone laughed—except Anne. He hadn't meant to stir up her fears—but he did. Anxiety rose in her chest.

Dear God, I don't know where I'm going—but You do. I have no place to call home. Please lead me, Lord. Help me trust You.

"Mr. Wilson, why are you headed to Oregon?" Logan asked.

"Well, I guess you could say life was getting pretty predictable. I thought there must be more a body could do in life besides just exist. I'd say God put a desire in me for more."

"So, where do you think this will lead?" Logan asked.

"I don't rightly know. Joining the army in mid-life does seem a bit crazy—but if they can use me, I'm happy to serve my country any way I can."

Surprisingly, Mrs. Wilson started to cry. Anne stepped over

rocks and pine cones to reach her side. Logan jumped up and brought a stump for Anne to sit on. Anne put her arm around her friend and asked, "What's wrong, Mrs. Wilson?"

Mrs. Wilson dabbed her tears with a corner of her skirt. "I miss my family…" With that, she burst out crying again.

"Your family?" Anne asked.

"I have three daughters and a son back in Missouri. I don't know if I'll ever see them again."

There was nothing anyone could say. Anne just held Mrs. Wilson as she cried. Twigs snapped in the fire—Mrs. Wilson sobbed—and Mr. Wilson coughed. There were no other sounds. All the night creatures hushed as if in sympathy.

Logan spoke up. "May I pray for you, ma'am?" Mrs. Wilson looked at him gratefully and nodded yes. With Anne on one side and Logan kneeling beside her on the other, the sobbing stopped and Mrs. Wilson relaxed.

"Dear Lord God, please comfort this precious woman. Thank You, Lord. Amen."

The next morning, the little group of travelers mushed their oxen into some of the most spectacular country Anne had ever seen. The snow-covered peaks were majestic. The mountains towered to unimaginable heights. Bighorn sheep could be seen grazing on the high, alpine meadows. Mountain goats looked like tiny dots on the mountain face.

Logan commented as he walked beside Anne, "I thought we had already seen the most beautiful landscapes—but this…" His breath came out in a long whistle.

The trail wound through an incredibly beautiful pass between the peaks, then suddenly plunged into a steep valley between huge firs and pines. The air was heavy with the fragrance of trees—and surprisingly—campfires. The valley was filled with smoke from dozens of campfires. Where had all these people come from? They were in the middle of nowhere.

A delegation of about ten Indian warriors on painted ponies blocked the trail. They were in full regalia—with bands of bright paint across their cheeks and spiked feathers in their hair.

The three wagons halted—of course—there were no other options. Two men rode up to the wagons. One of the men raised his hand as if he was offering a sign of peace. That's when the burned-out wagons farther down the trail could be seen.

Anne's thoughts ran wild. *Are they wanting to steal from us and burn our wagons? Will they scalp us and keep our hair as trophies? I remembered what Logan told me about wolves—don't show fear. These men remind me of ferocious wolves—ready to devour us. Oh God, help me not be afraid. Please protect us.*

One of the men beckoned with his hand for them to follow. Apparently, they were to leave the wagons and all they owned in the care of the rest of the delegation. Glancing back, Anne saw warriors climbing into the wagons. A verse burned in her heart. *Even though I walk through the valley of the shadow of death, I will fear no evil, for You are with me...*[18]

The warrior led the travelers into a tent covered in buffalo hides and badger skins. Deer and buffalo hides carpeted the floor. The tent was dark and smelled of smoked meat and sweetgrass. Their guide sat down and motioned they were to sit. A long pipe was lit and passed among the men. The Indians smiled. This seemed to be a gesture of peace.

All went well, until Mr. Wilson objected. He said he had never smoked in his life and didn't intend to start now. When the pipe was passed to him, he threw up his hands to say no. Immediately, Indian warriors put their hands on the knives tied to their chests by thick deerskin straps. Knives were pulled out of their sheaths.

Logan spoke calmly. "Mr. Wilson, if you don't smoke that pipe, you are a dead man—and we're probably all dead too."

Mr. Wilson obviously decided smoking was preferrable to death—so he took the pipe and inhaled deeply. Too deeply. His face turned green. The Indians watched him coughing and sputtering. Their faces looked like they didn't know whether to laugh or kill

---

[18] Psalm 23:4

him. Logan saw the looks on their faces, so he slapped Mr. Wilson on the back and laughed. That broke the tension and thankfully the Indians laughed too.

When the Indian guide motioned for them to follow, it wasn't clear where they were being led. *Will there be anything left in our wagons? Is my beautiful blanket Logan made for me lying on a buffalo hide in some tent? Is all our food gone?*

You can imagine the shock when the pioneers climbed into their wagons.

There were baskets of dried fish and mounds of tanned hides. A beautifully beaded deerskin dress was left in each wagon for the women. It was unbelievable.

Anne cried—partially because she felt her heart was so wicked—she had imagined all kinds of evil things about these kind people—and partially just from relief they were safe.

They searched for something—anything—to give as gifts. The women each donated a dress and a bag of flour. The men gave packages of matches and axes. The Indians had never seen matches, so the gifts appeared very valuable. As their painted, feathered friends waved goodbye, the little wagon train continued down the trail. Is all Anne could think was, *Thank You God for protecting us.*

Arriving at Fort Boise, the weary travelers saw a few soldiers huddled by the gate.

"Howdy folks," one of the soldiers called out. "Where are you heading?"

"Oregon City." Logan called back.

"Well, you best keep right on going," the soldier said.

"Why's that?"

"Smallpox. There's been an epidemic. Best keep moving."

Logan tried to mush the oxen a bit further. They stopped. It was obvious they were finished for the day. It was as if they were saying, "That's it. I'm done. Carry on without me."

"We may as well camp here," Logan said.

Logan smiled as he helped Anne down from the wagon.

In spite of the warmth of his smile, Anne suddenly felt chilled.

A fear—a foreboding—gripped her heart.

"Logan, something's wrong."

"What do you mean?"

"Remember when we were going to Devil's Gate—I asked if you ever have a feeling t something is about to happen—almost like God is warning you—telling you to prepare?"

"Yes, Why?"

"Cause that's how I feel now. Something's wrong."

CHAPTER SEVENTEEN

The Dalles, Oregon
July 1882

That night, a filthy hand clamped over Anne's mouth. She didn't have time to scream. The three desperate men wanted to take more hostages but decided one would be enough. They made their escape without alerting the other women.

Anne was dragged into the bushes, tied, gagged, and slung over a mule. The jarring seemed to go on forever. They finally stopped and rough hands pulled her to the ground. Ropes were pulled off.

Anne dusted off her skirt, stood as tall as she could, and demanded, "Why am I here?"

"Well, little missy, you're our ticket to freedom."

"Why?"

"That's enough jabbering. There's food waiting by the fire to be cooked. Get at it."

The man who appeared to be the leader slapped her across the backside, propelling her towards the place where another was building a fire.

Anne's face burned. *How dare he? Dear God, please protect me. Send Logan.*

When the men came back from filling the water barrels, Logan called Anne to tell her it would soon be time for supper. There was no reply.

A short time later he called again.

"Anne?"

By now it was getting dark.

"Anne?'

Logan got a torch and carried it to Anne's wagon. There were several large footprints—obviously not his—at the back of the wagon.

"Mr. Morgan! Mr. Wilson! Come quick!"

The men followed the tracks. Seeing a faint light in the distant hills, they extinguished their torches. As they got closer, they could see three men sitting near a fire. Anne was making dinner.

"This is wonderful!" one of the criminals said. "We have a cook—we will be safe from attacks. No soldiers or bounty hunters would dare shoot at us."

Logan spoke quietly. "I'll take the one with the beard."

Mr. Wilson said, "I'll take the bald guy."

"The fat guy's mine." Mr. Morgan said.

Logan spoke even quieter. "I will count to three. When I say three, we shoot."

"One…"

Anne walked in front of the men.

"No! Anne get out of the way!" Logan whispered.

Almost as if she heard him, she moved back towards the fire.

"…two, three!"

The criminals never knew what hit them.

"Anne!" Logan ran towards the terrified girl.

"Logan…" That was all she could say. She crumpled in his arms as he held her close.

"Anne…" he murmured into her hair.

Anne shook from the shock. Logan took off his jacket and wrapped it around her.

After Anne told the men what happened, Logan said, "I need to speak to the commander."

As they approached the fort, a soldier stood up and said, "You can't come any closer. Smallpox!"

Logan said, "I'm a US marshal and I need to speak to your commander."

The soldier said, "He can't be disturbed now."

"I said, I am a US marshal and I need to speak to your commander! Now!"

Logan spoke with such authority the soldier scurried into the fort.

The commander appeared and said, "What's this all about? My corporal says you are a US marshal."

"Yes, sir. Did you get a dispatch about three vicious criminals who escaped from a territorial prison?"

"I did. Why do you ask?"

"Well, sir, those men are lying on the hillside over yonder. They won't be bothering anyone again."

"What happened?"

"They kidnapped our Anne. They apparently planned to use her as a hostage. I thank God we found them."

"Well, I thank God too. What do you know about these men?"

"Not much. Just some information Anne heard while she was captive."

"Well, son, the leader of the group, Mr. Armstrong, was in a territorial prison near Fort Boise, doing time for manslaughter. While they worked in an orchard, he persuaded two fellow convicts to join him in overpowering their guards. The guards were knocked senseless and the criminals escaped. They hid in the foothills near Fort Boise."

"I assume they decided to find a hostage, to prevent the law from shooting at them. It might have worked—just too bad for them they chose Anne as their hostage," Logan said.

"Thanks for ridding the world of these scum. Where are you headed, son?"

"We'll be on our way to the Dalles in the morning."

"That's about a two-week trek. The Indians have been mighty hostile lately. I'll send some soldiers to accompany you."

"There's no need. We would attract less attention from the Indians as a smaller group. If there were soldiers the Indians could feel threatened and possibly attack."

"That's very wise, son. If you can handle Mr. Armstrong and his men, I'm sure you can handle most anything."

"Thank you, sir."

"I'd invite you in for dinner, but I'm sure my men informed you we are fighting smallpox at present."

"They told us. I pray God protects you."

"You too, son. God speed."

They walked back to the camp in silence. Mrs. Morgan and Mrs. Wilson were waiting impatiently by the fire. As soon as they saw Anne, they ran towards her. Mrs. Wilson cried from relief.

"Anne girl—oh dear Anne. Whatever happened?" Mrs. Morgan cried.

Anne was still in shock–all she could say was "…kidnapped."

"Oh Anne!" The women hugged her while thanking God she was safe.

It was nearly impossible for Anne to sleep that night. The crickets sounded noisier than usual. She heard someone walking outside the wagon.

"Logan?"

"Yes, Anne?"

"Thank you."

"Anne…"

"Yes?"

"I would give my life to protect you."

Anne couldn't reply. What does a person say to something like that? Finally, she could only whisper was, "Thank you."

Anne fell asleep basking in the knowledge she was protected— by God and Logan.

The next morning as they were about to leave, a group of soldiers arrived.

"We're looking for the marshal."

"You found him."

"The commander said to tell you he just found out there was a bounty on the men who were killed. The government has offered a reward—$1000 for each man—dead or alive."

Another soldier spoke. "The commander said when you arrive at Fort Dalles you are to speak to the government agent, Mr. Douglas T. Murphy. He will have the reward waiting for you and your men."

"Thank you."

The men praised God for His provision.

The journey to Fort Dalles was uneventful. The little group were thankful to be alive. Each day was considered a gift from God.

When they arrived at the fort, the men found hotel rooms where the women could bathe and sleep in proper beds. The men would sleep with the wagons and guard the animals to make sure they didn't disappear in the night.

The government agent's office was easy to find. Logan said to the man at the desk, "Hello. I'm looking for Mr. Douglas T. Murphy."

"May I ask why you are looking for him?"

"Yes. We are here to claim a bounty."

"And you are?"

"US Marshal Logan Mitchell. My friends and I are claiming the reward for shooting Mr. Armstrong and his men."

The clerk looked visibly shaken. "Right. I will tell Mr. Murphy you are here."

Mr. Murphy immediately appeared at a door and invited the men into his office.

"So, you are the men who shot the notorious Mr. Armstrong and his men? Did you know they had a reputation for being the most vicious criminals ever to have walked this Earth?"

"Can't say we knew that, Mr. Murphy. We were just rescuing our Anne—their hostage."

"Well now, I am pleased to give you each $1000 in appreciation by the US Government for your bravery and for ridding our country of these scum."

"Thank you, sir."

That night at dinner, the hotel manager sat with them to tell them how lucky they were.

"Now that you're safely past the hazards of the Great Plains and the mountains, you only have about a ten-day trek over Mount Hood on the Barlow Road to get to Oregon City."

Logan could see the relief on Anne's face. The man continued, "Yup. Just a few years back it would have been a different story."

"Why's that?" Mr. Wilson asked.

"Glad you asked. Just a few years ago, back in 1846, before Mr. Barlow cut a trail through the Cascade Mountains, the Columbia River was the only way to get to Oregon City."

"Everything a person owned had to be squashed onto a small wooden raft. It was a treacherous trip through raging rapids. The passage down the river was through a deep gorge with steep, sheer canyon walls. Many folks didn't make it."

"I can see why," Mrs. Wilson said.

"Yup. If an ox moved so much as a hoof, the raft could capsize and all would be lost. The bellowing of those oxen was heard echoing off the walls—making it sound like there was a whole herd going down the river."

"I'm thankful Mr. Barlow had a mind to find another route to Oregon City," Mrs. Morgan said.

The men thanked the hotel manager for all his information, said goodnight to the women, then turned to spend the night in the wagons. Logan looked forward to trying out the feather tick he had made for Anne. He wasn't one to complain, but a night off the hard ground sounded mighty fine.

That night, Anne's dreams were full of nightmares.

She saw Logan shoot her husband, saw the cross where her baby son Josiah was buried, and cried over Jeb leaving them so soon. She felt filthy hands grab her—then found herself on a wooden raft—bouncing off huge cavernous stone walls whose heights reached to heaven. The rapids were treacherous. She had to hang on. The raft capsized and she screamed as her body hit the frigid water.

Suddenly Mrs. Morgan was hovering over her—dressed in a petticoat—holding a coal oil lamp. Was she still dreaming? Mrs. Morgan looked at her kindly and stroked her hair as if Anne was a small child. "It's okay, Anne. You're fine. You were just having dreams. Go to sleep, sweet Anne-girl."

The next morning, after a lovely breakfast in the hotel, the little wagon train set off for the Barlow Trail. As the group passed the Columbia River, they were so thankful Mr. Barlow and his men hacked through the forest.

On the last night on the trail, as they sat by the fire, Logan asked, "What's wrong, Anne?"

Anne didn't speak at once. How could she tell this dear man what was really on her heart? How could she let him see him what a coward she really was?

"I'm afraid, Logan."

"Of what?"

"The unknown. The future..."

"Why are you afraid?"

"Ummm...maybe because I'm not trusting God."

Anne was surprised Logan didn't lecture her. He just quietly quietly watched the flames dance in the fire. Finally, he spoke. "I understand, Anne. You've gone through a lot."

"I'm sad our little family will be broken up. I might not see any of you again."

"That's a real possibility, Anne."

Did she dare say it? She decided he had to know. "I'll miss you, Logan."

Logan stared at the fire for the longest time. When he turned towards Anne, she was shocked to see tears in his eyes. "I'll miss you too, Anne."

Anne got up to spend her last night in the wagon.

"Good night, Logan."

Anne's breath caught in her throat.

Did he really just whisper, "Good night, my precious Anne?"

CHAPTER EIGHTEEN

So, this was Oregon City. Anne hurriedly walked down the boardwalk. She was to meet Logan in the hotel dining room for lunch and didn't want to be late. She adjusted her bonnet and smoothed the folds of her taffeta dress. It was the lovely blue dress Mrs. Morgan gave her back on the trail. She thought of her friends fondly. How sad the army had posted their husbands off in the wilds. Well, that was obviously where they were needed—but after being with them every day for months—it felt like she was missing her right arm.

Hurrying around a corner, Anne crashed into a giant of a man. "Pardon me, sir."

Anne didn't look at the man. She was too distracted—not wanting to keep Logan waiting.

"What's your hurry, little lady?"

Little lady? That voice... It can't be...

"Clayton?"

"Howdy, ma'am. Mighty fine to see you."

Anne looked up into the most evil eyes she had ever seen. They seemed to devour her. She almost said, "It's not mighty fine to see you." She decided not to antagonize the man. Instead, she just wordlessly stared at him.

"Cat's got your tongue, little lady? You must be so excited to see me you're speechless."

Anne tried to move around him, but the man sidestepped and blocked her path.

"Not so fast, Anne."

Hearing that man say her name almost made her hate it. He made it sound slimy, ugly…

"I have a proposal for you." Even Clayton's smile was ugly. He sneered through his crooked teeth.

"Please, sir, I have an appointment."

"You aren't going anywhere, Anne, until you hear my proposal."

It was obvious this man wasn't about to let her pass, so she reluctantly asked, "What's the proposal?"

Clayton grinned. It was a cat that's about to eat a canary grin. "Well, little lady. I hear you've fallen on hard times."

"Whoever gave you that information was speaking out of turn. God is providing for me."

"Ha. What does God have to do with anything?"

"Everything." Anne replied.

Clayton ignored her reply. "I am proposing marriage. I understand you have nothing. I am offering to provide for you and our children."

Anne fought the urge to vomit.

"I got a job as a blacksmith apprentice here in Oregon City. I have a room at the hotel. I'll soon have enough money to rent us a little house. What do you say?"

Anne looked incredulous. He had to be joking. She would starve to death before she would marry this man.

"Why are you offering this?" was all she managed to say.

"I knew from the moment I laid eyes on you I knew I wanted you more than any woman I've ever had."

Anne tried to think of a way to politely decline his offer and get away from the man.

"Clayton, thank you for your offer…"

Clayton stood grinning down into her face.

"…but I could never marry you."

His eyes squinted and grew dark.

"I could only marry for love…and I don't love you."

Clayton grabbed her arm as he hissed, "You can come willingly or my pistol can help convince you."

A pistol cocked behind him made Clayton freeze.

"You are under arrest for desertion from a US army post, aggravated assault, attempted kidnapping, possible murder, and uttering a death threat."

Anne had never seen Logan look so serious.

"Hands behind your back."

Logan snapped the handcuffs on Clayton and pressed the gun into his back as he said, "Move. Second door on your left."

"I'll get you for this, Logan."

"In your dreams. You aren't going to be breathing the air of freedom for a long time."

After the prisoner was deposited in the sheriff's office, Logan reached out his arm for Anne to hold. "Shall we?"

They walked towards the hotel in silence.

"That was quite enough excitement for one day." Logan said as he held the door open for Anne. He held her chair as she sat. Anne hadn't realized what a gentleman he was. There were no chairs on the trail.

Logan set his hat down on the table, poured a glass of water from the pitcher for Anne, and handed her a menu. "What do you feel like eating?"

"Honestly, I feel too upset to eat anything."

"Well, if I order something would you care to share it with me?"

"That's a great idea. Thank you, Logan."

Logan smiled at the man taking their order. "We would like a ham sandwich to share, please, and two large glasses of lemonade."

"How are you, Anne?"

What was it about this man that made her feel like she could tell him anything?

"I'm afraid, Logan."

She didn't mean to, but she started to cry softly. Logan reached over and took her hands in his.

They sat in silence.

The meal came.

They ate in silence.

Finally, Logan said, "I don't rightly know what to say, Anne, except trust God."

"I have a meeting with Judge Jenkins tomorrow morning at nine. It's right here. Would you meet him with me?"

"I'd be happy to be there for you, Anne."

Anne spent the rest of the afternoon applying at stores for work. The small amount of coins in her purse weren't going to last long.

"Hello, my name is Anne. I'm wondering if you need help here."

"What do you know about baking?"

"Well, I was a baker's assistant at Fort Laramie for six months."

"Well, to be honest, ma'am, I don't really need help now. If you come back at Christmas time, I reckon I could use an extra hand for a few weeks then."

It was the same at the mercantile, the dress shop, even in the hotel dining room. There was no need for her anywhere.

Okay, Lord, now what?

Anne felt God's voice gently whisper to her heart, *"Just be patient, Anne. Trust Me."*

That night, lying in a way too soft bed in the hotel, Anne thought about Logan.

He's such a good man, Lord. So caring. He is definitely the finest man I have ever met in my entire life. He has been such a good friend. I'm going to miss him when we part ways. He feels like family—like a brother—but somehow closer than a brother.

There was a loud explosion. Moments later, someone ran hollering down the hallway.

"FIRE! GET OUT NOW!!!"

Anne was thankful she hadn't had time to put her night shirt on. She quickly grabbed her carpet bag and ran to the door. The handle was too hot to touch. She hurried to the window and was relieved there was a staircase just outside the window.

Climbing out, she fell onto the landing and twisted her ankle. There was no time to be concerned about the pain. Anne hobbled down the stairs and stood behind the hotel, watching it burn. Logan appeared seemingly out of nowhere and grabbed Anne in a bear hug.

"Anne! You're safe! Thank God!"

"Logan…"

"I'm going to help fight the fire. Stay here. You're safe in this crowd."

A bucket brigade was quickly formed from the water pump to the hotel. Buckets of water were filled and passed down the line of volunteers. Hours later, thankfully, the fire was out. The exhausted volunteers were invited into the untouched dining room for a free drink of their choice. Logan asked for sarsaparilla. He carried his drink to the back of the hotel and offered it to Anne.

"Well, hopefully that's all the excitement we'll have for one night," Anne said.

"There's more, Anne. Somehow Clayton got the deputy's gun, shot him, and escaped. They've asked me to be the law here until they bring in a new sheriff."

"He escaped…?"

"Yup. I hate to be the one to tell you."

"Is the sheriff okay?"

"He lost a lot of blood, but he's going to live. I'll assign a guard to you, if you don't mind—just until Clayton has been captured."

Just then they heard the sound of a horse thundering towards them. They didn't have to look. They knew who it was.

"Drop your gun, marshal," a man hollered.

Logan pulled his gun out of the holster as if he was going to drop it—then quickly shot at the man on the horse. It happened too fast for Clayton to do anything. He fell off the horse, writhing on the ground. His hand was mangled.

"Well Clayton, you are under arrest again. This time we are adding the criminal act of arson—trying to burn down the hotel— to your list of crimes."

"How do you know it was me?"

"Maybe when you escaped from the jail, you shouldn't have taken sticks of dynamite and matches with you."

Logan marched Clayton to the jail and locked him in the cell. Anne walked with them. She looked at the man huddled on the bed, crying because of the pain in his hand—the pain in his life. Anne didn't see an evil, hulking man—she saw someone God greatly loved.

"May I speak to the prisoner, Logan?"

"As you wish, Anne."

Anne touched the bars as she spoke.

"Clayton?"

Clayton sat rocking on the cot, holding his bandaged hand. He lifted his eyes and looked at Anne through a haze of pain.

"Clayton, I want you to know God loves you—and I forgive you."

He looked like he was trying to comprehend what was being said.

"If you ask God to forgive you—even though in the eyes of the law you are still guilty—in God's eyes you'd be a free man."

"How can you forgive me?" Clayton muttered. Nastiness edged his voice.

"I can only forgive you, because I realize how much God has forgiven me."

Clayton stared at the floor—apparently not sure what to say.

Anne was surprised to see a tear fall from his eye. Was it because he was sorry—or was he sorry he was caught?

"Clayton, there is none righteous. No, not one. We have all sinned and fall short of the glory of God. We all need His forgiveness and amazing grace."

There was a long silence. Anne wasn't sure if her words were having any effect.

"Anne, I've wronged you. I'm sorry."

Then, as if a dam broke in his heart, Clayton started to howl. "Oh God, I've wronged You. I'm so sorry. Forgive me."

He looked at Anne through his tears. It was real. The dark evil that had dwelt in his eyes was gone. In their place were the innocent eyes of a newborn child.

"You're forgiven, Clayton. By God and by me. Don't waste the time you have left. Live for God. I hope to meet you in Heaven one day, brother."

CHAPTER NINETEEN

Oregon City
July 1882

"That was quite the night," Anne said as they walked towards the hotel.

Logan grinned at her. "You've got that right. It seems adventure follows you."

"Thank you for agreeing to meet Judge Jenkins with me."

The wind blew softly, carrying the scent of baby apples on the breeze. Logan reached over and gently moved a lock of hair off Anne's face.

"I was glad to be there for you. Now we just have to wait to see what he decides about your case. It's a pretty unusual case. How does one decide what to do with several stolen gold bars worth thousands of dollars?"

"I'm afraid, Logan."

"There's nothing to be afraid of, Anne."

"Yes, there is, Logan. I'm afraid of what will happen to me."

"Anne, you have nothing to fear. God will take care of you."

"But what if He doesn't?"

"Trust Him, Anne. He loves you."

"It's easier to believe that for someone else."

"I understand, Anne. But you told the judge the truth—the whole story—right from when I rode up to your camp—right from when William was killed. You showed him the wanted posters. It's all up to God now."

"I am trusting God the judge will decide what's best."

"Judge Jenkins is a good man—an honest man. He will decide what happens to the gold…the wagon…the oxen…the supplies."

"The wagon and supplies? I hadn't thought about them. So—I could be left with nothing?"

"You could. Or you could end up a very rich woman."

The next morning Judge Jenkins met with Anne and Logan in the hotel dining room. He asked questions while chewing on his bacon and eggs.

"Will you join me?" The judge smiled at Anne.

"Thank you, sir, but I'm honestly too nervous to eat."

The judge looked solemn as he asked, "So, Anne, you knew nothing of William Ryan's past?"

"No, sir."

"You had no questions about where the money came from to outfit your wagon for the trip?"

"Honestly, sir, that thought never crossed my mind."

"When did you find out about the gold bars? Tell me again."

"I found them when Marshal Logan shot the lock off William's trunk. I was looking for gifts to give the kind Indians who helped us."

"And tell me again, why did you come forward with this information?"

"Because I want to do what's right, sir. If the people who were stolen from have their money returned, I think that would only be fair."

"But, you will have nothing."

Anne smiled. "Marshal Logan has been helping me understand that God loves me and will take care of me. I have decided to trust

Him—no matter what is decided today."

"Well, Miss Anne, I'm going to deliberate on your case further today. I've sent a wire to my friend—an excellent lawyer in Chicago. I have asked his opinion of the legality of this case. He promised to get back to me today. Could you meet me here at dinner time? Say, six o'clock?"

"Of course."

"I will have an answer for you then."

As they walked into the sunshine, Logan said, "The mayor is swearing in a new deputy today. I'm not needed. Would you like to go for a picnic? I can get some bread and cheese."

"That would be lovely, Logan. Thank you."

They walked to the bakery and got a loaf of sourdough bread. The mercantile had a slab of aged cheddar that smelled divine. Logan picked up some jars to fill with water and a couple of apples and dried figs.

"There's a pretty waterfall just down the road. Do you want to walk or should I rent a buggy?"

"It's a beautiful day for a walk."

When they arrived at the waterfall, Logan took off his jacket for Anne to sit on. He filled the jars with the clear water gushing by them.

"I hate to sit. I'm going to crush these gorgeous wildflowers."

"I'm sure they won't mind. There's a beautiful wildflower sitting on them."

"Logan...stop teasing me."

"I mean it, Anne."

He looked at Anne so earnestly she had to look away.

"If you could have anything in this world—what would it be?"

"I can't answer that, Logan."

"Why?"

"Because I have agonized over that very question for months."

"Well, there's no harm in telling me."

Anne's eyes filled with tears. "There would be a lot of harm, Logan. I know I can never have the thing I want most, so I have to let that dream die. I'm sorry I can't tell you."

They sat in silence. The bread, cheese and fruit untouched.

"Can't you eat anything, Anne?"

"No."

"Anne, I'm heading out in the morning. I'm very glad I could spend this last day with you."

"You're leaving?" She tried to blink them away but tears kept forming in her eyes.

"Yes. I'm not needed here. I'll be looking for a posting in one of the settlements."

"I'm sad to see you go."

"I'll miss you, Anne. You've been a precious sister...a friend...and more to me."

"Thank you, Logan."

"We still have a few hours before we have to meet the judge. I brought some fishing line and hooks. Would you like to go fishing?"

"I'd love to. Try not to catch another gopher."

They both laughed.

"That was funny—but obviously not to the poor gopher."

As they walked to the hotel with three fat trout on a string, Logan broke the silence.

"Anne, I'm really going to miss you."

"I'm really going to miss you, Logan."

When they arrived at the hotel, Logan gave the trout to the cook with instructions to fry them in salted butter.

"Judge Jenkins, we caught some lovely trout today. Would you join us for dinner?"

"I'd be happy to, son."

"Now, about this case..."

Anne held her breath.

"My friend in Chicago said in this case there is no way to determine who the money actually belongs to. He ruled, and I agree, the gold is yours."

Anne let out her breath, then burst out crying.

"My dear, I thought this would be happy news..."

"It is…" Anne cried.

The judge looked at Logan, raised his eyebrows and said, "Women. Impossible to understand."

"Oh, I understand," Logan said. "She was carrying so much fear of the future—now she is feeling the weight lifting off her shoulders. Is that right, Anne?"

Anne couldn't answer. She just nodded yes.

"It's okay, Anne." Logan smiled and held her hand. She immediately felt his comfort…his concern…his love.

"What will you do now, Miss?"

"Well, I've been thinking I'd love to build a home—on a ranch."

"That's a mighty big dream, Anne."

"I've been dreaming of it for months. It's what I'd like more than anything in the world."

"Pardon me for asking, Anne—but how will you take care of a ranch by yourself?"

"Well, that's the problem with that dream, Judge. I'd have to find a strong man to manage the ranch. Someone with the same dream."

She didn't dare look at Logan. She kept looking at the judge—smiling at his approving nod.

Logan finally spoke. "Anne, I'd be willing to be your ranch manager."

Anne turned to look at him. "But what about being a US marshal? Wouldn't you miss that?" She already knew the answer, but she wanted to hear him say it.

"Anne…"

Logan got down on his knee. He looked like a knight, kneeling before a maiden, vowing to protect and cherish her.

"Will you marry me? I love you, Anne girl."

Anne burst out crying again.

"Logan, that is the one thing I wanted more than anything but couldn't tell you because I thought I could never have it. I love you too."

"Well, we just happen to have a judge here. Would you be kind enough to marry us?" Logan asked.

"Well folks, I'm leaving in the morning. It would have to be now."

Logan stood and spoke to all present in the dining room. "Folks, I have just asked this beautiful, precious woman to be my wife. She said yes."

Cheers went up from about two dozen people.

"Judge Jenkins kindly said he would marry us…right now. I would like to invite you all to be witnesses."

Another cheer went up from the crowd.

Judge Jenkins stood solemnly. He said wedding vows were not to be taken lightly. They were meant to bind a couple to God and each other all the days of their lives.

Anne was giddy with excitement. *Logan has asked me to be his wife? Lord, how amazing! You knew, didn't You, Lord?*

She looked at Logan. He smiled at her—his heart-warming, breathtakingly beautiful smile. His eyes were full of love—and more—joy and thankfulness.

"Folks, we are gathered together today to join this man and this woman in Holy matrimony."

Marriage? Logan is going to be my husband? God, You are amazing! Completely, totally, and utterly amazing!

"… and forsaking all others, keep only to him as long as you both shall live?"

Am I dreaming, Lord? This can't be real…

"Anne, are you going to answer the question?"

"Yes! Yes, of course… what was the question?"

"Will you marry this man and forsake all others?"

"YES!"

"To have and to hold, from this day forward…"

He will be my husband. I can hold him any time…

"For better or for worse, for richer, for poorer, in sickness and in health, to love and to cherish, until death do us part."

"Amen. I mean yes!" Anne said.

"Yes!" Logan repeated. "Oh Anne, this is a dream come true. I could never love another as much as I love you."

"You may kiss your bride."

His bride! Logan's bride! That's me! Oh God, You are so good! Thank You!

Logan held his bride as if he would never let her go. All in the room cheered.

"Thank You, God!" he murmured into her ear. "Thank You for this beautiful, precious woman. My wife…"

EPILOGUE

What joy accompanied the wedding of Anne Ryan and Logan Mitchell. Theirs was a love that was born out of deep respect, honor, kindness, humility, and purity. It was a match made by God.

They found a magnificent piece of land in Oregon's Willamette Valley. Logan thanked God daily for giving him his heart's desire—a wife, a family, a home. Speaking of family, they raised eleven children. Logan said they were so beautiful because they looked so much like their mother.

Anne dropped all charges against Clayton. Surprisingly, he became a circuit preacher. God so transformed his life he wanted to tell others about God's amazing grace.

The Morgans settled into a lovely house in Oregon City.

The Wilsons never felt at home in Oregon. The grief Mrs. Wilson felt over the loss of her children convinced Mr. Wilson they needed to go back to Missouri. They made the trip across the continent in 1884 by train. The trip took just over one week.

They all were looking for a place of belonging—a place called home.

God created a hunger in our hearts for home. He is the only one who can fulfil that desire. He is creating a beautiful home for you to live in forever—a place where there is no longer pain or suffering—a place of love, beauty, and purity.

There is so much more than you are experiencing now waiting for you. You know there's more. God has set eternity in your heart. I pray God holds you close—and leads you safely through this world to Your Heavenly home.

PREVIOUS PRAIRIE ROSES COLLECTIONS

Ella
NANCY FRASER

Calli
DONNA SCHLACHTER

Laney
VICKIE McDONOUGH

Sabra
PATRICIA PACJAC CARROLL

2022 COLLECTION

Pearl
ZINA ABBOTT

Glory
MARISA MASTERSON

Rose
RENA GROOT

Aria
MONDA CZESCHIN FISCHER

Elsie
KC HART

Amity
LINDA CARROLL BRADD

Amy
ANGELA LAIN

Jo
CARYL McADOO

Acknowledgements

Thank You, Lord God, for putting this book on my heart.
I acknowledge that without you I can't even take my next breath.
Thank You for the ideas for Anne.

Thank you, Caryl McAdoo, for inviting me to be part of this beautiful collection with so many gifted authors. Thank you for patiently helping me learn how to be a writer in a book collection.

Thank you to all my editors,
my amazing Advanced Copy Readers…
Kim Christopher Bushong, Evelyn Foreman, LoRee Peery,
Linda Hobson, Debbie Curto, Leanne Paetkau,
Steve Clement, Linda Martin, Loretta Eidson, Renee Simmons,
Linda Leibel, Dawn Legros, Seanna-Marie Phillips,
Phyllis Rundell, Barby Molnar, Becky Smith,
Jessica Grewe, Lisa Turley, Pam Harvey, David Balfour,
Gail Clarke, Trudy Cordle, Becky Ramsay, Kathy Hart,
Kristin Carmack, Rachel Lilley, Debra Holley, Debra Sonnichsen,
Cindi Snow, Judith Hall, Myrna Peters, Michelle Roden,
Diane Brown, Karyn Neenan, Kathleen McCune, Betty Vander
Wier, Lyn Town, and Shonda Fischer.
I appreciate you all so much!

Thank you, Randi Gammons, for the gorgeous cover design and
Delia Latham for formatting this book and making it look
beautiful.

All of Rena's Titles

Author's Note

Dear Reader,

Thank you for reading my novel. You have only a certain number of hours in this life, and you shared some of them with me. I am honored.

I hope you found Anne gave God glory and spoke to your heart about His amazing love. The details in this story describing the Oregon Trail are true. It was a miracle anyone survived the grueling trip.

Reviews are so important to authors, so if you enjoyed this story, would you please take the time to leave a quick review at <u>Amazon</u>, <u>Goodreads</u>, Bookbub, your blog, or anywhere you enjoy reading about books. Of course, tell your friends. Stop by my <u>Facebook</u> page. I love connecting! The links are on the next page.

I pray that God will bless you, that His loving kindness and favor will envelop you, now and forever!

Blessings,

Rena Groot

About the Author

Ever since she walked into her first-grade classroom as a little awe-struck girl, Rena dreamed of being a school teacher. Dreams do come true. She earned a Bachelor of Education from the University of Alberta and a Masters of Religious Education from the Southern Baptist Seminary in Cochrane, Alberta.

Rena has been a teacher in Canada and China. She wrote *A Life Set Free* under a mosquito net in China. That's when her addiction to writing was born.

God has given her the honor of being an ambassador with "The Department of Eternal Affairs" to so many cool places ~ Haiti, a jungle village in Belize, the Ghetto in NYC, behind the Iron Curtain in Poland and Romania, in Israel, China, Thailand, Mexico, Canada, Africa, and Greece. She started a blog to bless, encourage, and sometimes challenge people. Here's the links.

- renagroot.com (blog)
- renagroot@yahoo.ca (email)
- https://amzn.to/376xOrv (Amazon)
- https://www.facebook.com/rena.groot
- Broken to Beautiful—Transformed by God's Power (online course coming soon)

Made in the USA
Las Vegas, NV
17 January 2024